You'll Never Walk Alone

Daniel Lissamore

Published in 2021 by Tales From the Kop Publishing

Dedications

To my family especially my father and brother, who are sadly no longer with us, but well and truly alive within the pages of this book. To my Mum, who loves every story I write, including the rubbish ones, and to the ninety-six people (who have sadly become ninety-seven since I began writing this) who lost their lives on 15th April 1989.

You'll Never Walk Alone.

Prologue

Ezra Kennedy

8th March 2020

I stopped going to Anfield after it happened, choosing to spend my Saturday afternoons on a different kind of *Onion Patch*. My allotment. To say they were the happiest days of my life would be remiss under the circumstances, but they were the days I came closest to finding peace.

Listen! Behold, a sower went out to sow. And as he sowed, some seed fell along the path, and the birds came and devoured it. Other seed fell on rocky ground, where it did not have much soil, and immediately it sprang up, since it had no depth of soil. And when the sun rose, it was scorched, and since it had no root, it withered away. Other seed fell among thorns, and the thorns grew up and choked it, and it yielded no grain. And other seeds fell into good soil and produced grain, growing up and increasing and yielding thirtyfold and sixtyfold and a hundredfold." And he said, "He who has ears to hear, let him hear."

Mark 4:3-9

In my experience, even those who've never set foot inside a church have usually heard the parable of the sower. At some point or another, they've probably wondered which soil their seeds landed in. But not me. You could compare me to

1

the sower himself. The man who spread the word of God. Still, the more I thought about the parable of the sower, the more I understood it. That story about seeds and soil was not only true when talking about faith. It also explained my grief and the grief of those around me. When I thought about it that way, there were days when I felt the scorching sun on my back. Years, maybe. But in the end, I would look at the family I had left and return to sowing my seeds.

I wish the same could be said of my wife, Susan. Sadly, her suffering was much greater than mine. After all, there's no bond stronger than a mother and her child. Her grief landed in thorns so sharp they robbed her of her faith. Not just in God, but her faith in me. That's the other reason I spent more time on my allotment after ar Kenny died. I couldn't bear how I'd let her down. The irony of it all, as a man of God who toiled to heal the pain of others, I'd completely failed to protect my own. But despite those brambles being thicker than barbed wire, despite her crop being strangled time and time again, my Susan fought back with thorns of her own. Despite everything, she remained the brightest flower in my garden. My wild rose. That's why I loved her, above all else. That's why I knew she would be by my side, as I magnificently sailed into the mystic.

Chapter 1

Wayne Kennedy

11th March 2020

As we swerved the rocket, or left the M62 if you're a total *wool*, the endless drone of Richie's new *leccy* motor finally became unbearable. I won't deny how smooth it all felt at first, but two-hundred and twenty miles later and the lack of grunt was completely suffocating, a constant reminder how the gulf between us was wider than the Mersey. For the past four hours, our attempt at conversation had been more embarrassing than watching a bunch of blue-noses trying to emulate the expansive football of Jürgen Klopp under their new blocker, Carlo Ancellotti. Sure, there'd been a couple of sideways passes, a few attempts to move the ball forward, only to be followed by another long ball back to the goalkeeper. It wasn't all ar Richie's fault. It was me who was stuck in the past. In many ways, I was like the fuel-burning cars in our rear-view mirror, left behind to dawdle in the slow lane.

I realised people spoke differently nowadays, certain topics were no longer acceptable, so I think ar Richie was trying to appease me when he told me this one story, somewhere on the outskirts of Manchester. Apparently, he took some pretty intern over to United last week. This *Judy* was not only half his age, she had these long legs and them *up-de-entry* eyes. It seems he only had to mention how his passion wagon could pretty much drive itself, whilst saving both the rainforests and the polar bears and she couldn't contain herself any longer. A simple stroke of her inner thigh and she became as randy as a butcher's dog. By all accounts, he didn't even need to pull over. Now, even I knew he was having trouble in his marriage, but I couldn't help but wonder whether there was a *clean-the-seats-after-sex-mode* operated somewhere on the huge screen at the centre of the dashboard, which was bigger than the telly in ar front room when we were kids.

I'm not sure if this is entirely politically correct either, but let's just say I assumed ar Richie enjoyed being hugged a little too much after he scored a goal when we were growing up. Not that it would've mattered, providing his boyfriend hadn't turned out to be a Toffee. So all things considered, I was pretty relieved he was finally getting a bit of action with the ladies, it's just with everything going on, I really didn't need this type of enforced intimacy, least of all with my little *whacker* of a brother. Not only was ar arl Fella in the *ozzy*, but it was Champions League Semi-Final night. Ar Richie had only refused to keep the radio on for the pre-match news, insisting the real joy of driving electric was the

4

contemplative silence. He did allow us a couple of tunes on something called *Spotify,* in a traffic jam a few miles south of Birmingham. Apparently, it's some kind of artificial intelligence *tingey,* which can tell what kind of music you like without even meeting you. I guess it wasn't that intelligent, otherwise it would've known that *King of Kings* might've represented a return of form for *Echo and the Bunnymen,* but it couldn't be compared to *Villiers Terrace,* not by a long-chalk. It was just one of many occasions when we could've had a right *laff,* if only ar Richie didn't always assume everything *auld* was proper *antwacky.*

It was Ma who insisted I travel down to London, so I could sit beside her prodigal son like a guardian angel on his return. Or maybe it was the other way round. What she really wanted was for us to do some male bonding along the way. With my arl Fella's condition taking a grave swerve for the worse, I couldn't really refuse her, not without explaining the inner workings of Richie's futuristic fanny magnet. She definitely wasn't ready for that story, although I doubt she'd have believed me anyway. The only car her and my arl Fella ever owned was a beige Austin Allegro with a brown vinyl roof, which was tragically torn to shreds by the baboons at Knowsley Safari Park. It's wholesome memories like that which made me wonder where it all went wrong. You certainly can't lay fault at my Ma or my arl Fella's door for how we've drifted apart. The event which caused *that* was far bigger than all of us.

Richie was only fifteen when it happened. That in itself should've been enough to forgive him, but it didn't hide the truth. Over thirty years had passed and other than the fact we were both born at the same *ozzy* on Mill Road, birthed by the same *Judy*, we had nothing in common. I don't think ar Richie ever reached out to me, not since he left Merseyside. Sure, we'd crossed paths on the odd occasion, when I still had the coppers to travel down South for away games. But we never planned to meet. We didn't even go to the footy together. Despite his job, I'm not sure Richie really understood the game. Of course he could explain the madness of a VAR decision and he knew who was worth what and whether they might be unsettled in their current contract. He was an absolute legend at negotiating them a new deal, providing he got his slice of the slosh. But ask him who was the better finisher out of John Aldridge and Ian Rush, or who was the better passer of the ball out of Ronnie Whelan and Jan Molby and he wouldn't have a *scooby*.

You could say it was a score-draw if you want, after all we're talking about Saturday afternoons, in crowded pubs, amidst the frenzy of match day. On most occasions it wasn't even possible to stop, with me being swept along in a sea of red towards the turnstiles and him trudging past with a total cobb on, his head buried in some *Apple* or *BlackBerry*. Having said all that, I still blame my totally *brewstered* little brother. I understand how going to the footy might've felt like a busman's holiday in his line of work, but he knew Liverpool's away fixtures just as well as I did. He could've easily used one of them fruit-flavoured gizmos to arrange a jolly after the game, to raise a glass to *auld* times and sink some *bevvies*. Take this road trip for instance, having come all the way down on a National Express coach, just to sit next to him so he didn't have to drive up here alone, he still didn't invite me into his poxy flat. Instead, we had to meet at some charging station down the road, which looked like something out of *Star Wars*. It's not that I begrudged him doing well for himself, or that he'd become a total whacker (and trust me he had become a total whacker.) It just felt like he'd been socially distancing, long before it was a thing, scared to let anything from Liverpool into his new life, in case it got contaminated.

'Check out that,' I said, as we swung past de Mizzy in Wavertree. 'Me and Kenny both put a few goals past you there.' But Richie didn't respond. Maybe he was too embarrassed. He just swept his finger deftly over his precious

7

touchscreen, turning it back into a giant map, and I started to wonder if he still knew the way home.

There was talk earlier in the day about the game being cancelled because of the dreaded coronavirus, but by the time we got to Toxteth you could tell it was still on. Sure, the real action was a couple of miles across town, but the pubs and take-aways had that unmistakable buzz about them, red scarves draped across the windows and *bladdered Kopites* swaying in the streets. By now, I was desperate to get out and join them. Despite being one down from the first-leg, there was a confidence in the air. After all, it was only Atletico Madrid, not the mighty Real, and tonight they'd got to come to the *Onion Patch*, home of the champions of Europe. I'd be shocked if they could turn us over in our own backyard.

Not as shocked as I was when Richie decided to pull over in the little lay-by across the street from the *Royal*. Not the one they knocked down on the corner of Admiral Street, the other one opposite the cemetery. If you think I was worried about some *blert chiefing* the *Deli Ali's* off ar Richie's new motor then you're having a laugh. I've been a *Tockie* all my life and, trust me when I tell you, you've been watching too much Harry Enfield my son. I just didn't expect him to come past this way, that's all, let alone stop.

8

My legs felt like jelly as I finally stood up, so I did a little jig to shake them loose and Richie did the same. It was almost like a pre-match warm-up, before Richie grabbed some *bevvies* from the boot and followed me through the *auld* iron gates. Don't ask me why, but the moment my feet touched that gravel path, I started to peg it. We both did. Just for a second it was like *auld* times, the holy trinity *sagging* off *skewl*, scarpering across St Agnes Field on a Friday afternoon. Kenny and Richie keeping *douse* on the corner, whilst I nipped to the offy with my *jarg ID* and came out clutching a packet of *ciggies* and a bottle of *White Lightening*. Those were the days, when *plazzy* bags were free and you could still get ten players for under a quid.

As always, I completely left Richie for dead. He couldn't catch a pig in a *jigger* that one. Still, what he lacked in speed he made up for with cheating. In that way, he was both a prima donna and a Maradona. As I negotiated the tight bend through the wind-clipped trees, the spawny git took a shortcut across the old war graves. Fair enough, but a bit disrespectful if you ask me. By the time I caught him at ar Kenny's memorial, he was bent over, hands on his knees, taking huge gasps of air between fits of hacking coughs. 'What's up with you?' I asked, a little worse for wear myself. 'Don't the *bizzies* chase you down south?'

'Something like that,' he said, cracking open one of them beer cans and offering the other one to me. 'Are you having one? I never know with you.'

'Go on then,' I said, mustering a bit of fake resistance. 'Even the Doc said I shouldn't give up all at once.' That bit was at least true. On my last appointment he even prescribed me a couple of those little bottles of red, with just a *willy-dribble* inside, advising me to stick to one a day so my liver didn't go into shock. I kept it up for about two days, before I swapped them for the big bottles. Although truth be told, I'd already sunk two of them on the coach down here. After all, I needed something to take the edge of things if I was going to spend the whole day with this little whacker.

'I really miss him,' Richie said, standing over Kenny's memorial and putting an arm around my shoulder. 'I miss the both of you.'

To say it caught me off guard was a bit of an understatement. It was like the eighty-eight FA Cup Final all over again. I was Liverpool, blessed with proper players like Aldridge, Houghton and Barnes. Although, as my arl Fella would've said, without the likes of Steve McMahon they wouldn't have had the freedom to go forward. Anyway, I'd spent the past thirty years slowly pushing the ball around to paint a picture of ar Richie as this total *plazzy* scouser and he'd completely undone me. A giant hoof into the box, a glancing header at the near post and it was *Lawrie bloody Sanchez* all over again.

Now, I didn't know what to say. Having spent the last three decades hardly speaking, suddenly it was all a bit too much. Part of me was angry. Another part was proper confused. In the end, I just blurted out the first thing which came into my head. 'Don't get down the banks *La*, we can still make kick-off if we try.'

Chapter 2
Wayne Kennedy
11th March 2020

We got back on the road and almost as far as Edge Hill before the traffic ground to a standstill. Twenty minutes until kick-off and we were stuck behind some *blert* on a bicycle. Let's get this straight, I've no problem with people cycling to work. I'm all about saving the environment, or even the bus fare for that matter, but this whacker was a complete MAMIL (middle-aged man in lycra.) I've got Liverpool shirts dating back to eighty-nine, the red one covered in little white triangles with *Candy* written across the chest. So you'd have thought I'd pally up to this *meff*, parading around in his team's colours and everything. But this was just another one of those things which was different these days. Tell me what was wrong with the baggy *Adidas* shell-suits we used to wear to ride our *Raleigh Grifters* around *Tockie*. It wasn't a loose-fitting pair of trackie bottoms this *blert* should've been worried about, it was the saddle bags around his midriff that were slowing him down. Add a poxy helmet into the mix and he looked like a condom with advertising space. To make matters worse, he stood up in the saddle and started waving his arse from side to side. Now, I didn't want to look, but it was right on the end of my nose, like somebody trying to smuggle a couple of pickled onions in a leather purse. 'Shame this car of yours doesn't have a rocket launcher, Rich,' I said, tapping away at the giant screen on the dashboard. 'You could be like Knight Rider and blow his bloody bollocks off.'

Despite it being ar kid's favourite show growing up, he didn't take it too well. 'For fuck sake how many times do I need to tell you? Don't touch anything.'

I should have known the false pretences we'd been sharing in the cemetery wouldn't amount to much, but at least his car seemed to get the message. Without ar Richie doing anything, it took a sharp right down Wavertree Road, leaving that bloody cyclist well behind. Not that it did us much good, a swarm of B*izzies* came pouring out the station, holding up the traffic as they crossed the street. It wasn't until we branched left I realised we weren't following them over to the *Onion Patch*.

'Anfield's that way, Rich,' I said, pointing up Low Hill. 'You better take over the wheel again.'

'For fuck's sake Wayne. There's more to life than football,' he snapped.

'Don't let Shankly hear you say that,' I replied, crossing my chest and forehead, like a proper *Farder Bunloaf*. 'God rest his soul.'

'Oh, is that right?' Richie said, sarcastically. 'This'll be good.'

I coughed up a bit of phlegm to the back of my throat, so I sounded just like the big man. 'Football is not a matter of life and death. I can assure you, it is much, much more important than that.'

Richie shook his head, dismissively. 'I'm well aware of the reference. But it's a misquote. I thought everyone knew that. He never meant it to be taken literally.'

'Of course he did.' By now I could feel my blood rising. 'How else could he have fucking meant it?'

'I forget the exact words, but what he actually said was he felt sorry for people like that. He was on the verge of being replaced by Paisley and he was reflecting on the way he was being treated by the board.'

'Don't butt in with the men,' I replied. 'That's complete and utter bollocks and you know it.'

'Okay Wayne.' Richie smiled. 'I don't want a row, but there's been a tonne of articles about it on the internet.'

'Too right, you don't want a row, you little whacker!' I shouted. 'We both know how that would end.'

'There's no need to get *airyated*,' he replied, holding his palms up defensively.

15

'Trust me pal. You'd know if I was *airyated*. Now, are you gonna drive us to the footy or not?' I asked.

'I thought that was obvious,' Richie said. 'I set it up to take us over to the *ozzy* to visit the arl Fella. Wasn't that why we met in the first place?'

'And we will.' I said. 'After the match.'

Richie rolled his eyes in disbelief. 'Visiting hours will be over by then.'

And that's when I let it slip. 'I'm sure when Ma asked me to come and get you, what she really wanted was for us to make amends.'

'And suddenly the truth comes out.' Richie jabbed his index finger hard into my chest. 'You only came because she told you to. I bet she's still paying for your season ticket, isn't she?'

'So what if she is?' I said, although truth be told, it was a bit of a sore point. Forty-eight years-old and my Ma still had to pay for me to go out with my mates.

'That's the thing with you, Wayne. It's football first and family second. It always has been and always will be.'

'Fuck off!' I exclaimed, unable to listen to much more of this bullshit.

'No, let's be really honest,' Richie said, continuing to berate me. 'It's alcohol first, football second and fuck knows where family fits in.'

'And that's coming from the brother who's been away so long he needs a fucking sat-nav to find Toxteth cemetery.'

'You know I was just putting it into self-drive mode.' Richie said confidently, like he actually believed his own bullshit. 'And I come back when I can. It's just I've got a life and a job in London. You should try it sometime.'

'I've got a life!' I shouted, driving my fist into his precious dashboard. 'Right here, keeping this family together.'

'Sponging off them, more like,' Richie replied.

'Pull this car over right now,' I screamed. 'Or you'll be arriving to see the *arl Fella* in the back of an ambulance.'

'Fine.' Richie said, stamping hard on the brakes. 'And what should I tell Ma? Did little Wayne do enough to get his pocket money?'

'Tell her I sat with you as far as Low Hill,' I said, opening the car door. 'But I couldn't put up with your pious bullshit for a second longer.'

I couldn't believe what I'd just heard as I headed out into a line of blaring traffic. Didn't he understand this was my family. This was where I felt closest to Kenny. As I crossed

17

the Erskine roundabout, I must've still been turning the air blue. Not that anybody cared. By then I was lost in an army of red shirts, chanting as we marched up West Derby Road.

If you're tired and you're weary,
And your heart skips a beat,
You'll get your fucking head kicked in,
If you walk down Heyworth Street,
If you come to The Albert,
You'll hear our famous noise,
Get out you Everton bastards,
We're the Billy Shankly Boys.

We got as far as Oakfield before the heavens opened, which probably did me a favour. My shirt was stuck to my back by the time I took my seat behind the goal, but at least I'd calmed down. Rain was lashing across the pitch and Anfield was more like a port in a storm than a football stadium, a sea of red ready to watch Klopp's navy go to war with the armada from Madrid.

The official attendance was announced at fifty-two thousand, two hundred and sixty-seven. But take it from me, they were wrong. They always are. Even when it's a full-house, there's always more fans than they think. Ninety-six of them to be precise, stood at the Kop-end for every game since eighty-nine, even though it's an all-seater these days, cheering on the reds from beyond the grave.

Despite our best efforts, the boys got off to a horrible start. Atletico caught us napping from the kick-off. A clever pass from Felix and Costa got in behind Gomez. His low shot shaved the outside of Adrián's post, who looked beaten for a moment. The keeper held his hands aloft, trying to make out he had it covered in a vain attempt to settle things down before he took the goal kick. I think we all would've felt safer with Allison between the sticks, but he still hadn't recovered from the injury which kept him side-lined at the weekend. Adrián was no Bruce Grobbelaar, and he wasn't even wearing the number one jersey, but tonight he'd have to do.

We survived the early barrage, before last season's hero started to shine. A finely weighted cross from Trent Alexander-Arnold found the Dutchman's head on the edge of the six-yard box, but Wijnaldum's glancing header always seemed destined for the keeper's arms. At least we were shaping now.

First Salah cut inside his man and sent a speculative effort high and wide. Then the skipper missed a half-chance which might have made things square. Their keeper was already a contender for man of the match by the time Oxlade-

Chamberlain stung his palms with a low drive. Unfortunately, the rebound trickled away to safety.

We earned a couple of corners for our efforts, both of which threatened their goal. The first forced some last ditch defending, only to see the ball put behind for another. The second one was an even sweeter delivery, which found Mane only six-yards out. He headed it goalwards and it appeared to hit a defender's hand before it bounced away. 'Penalty!' I screamed, but the ref waived away any protests, including mine.

When the half-hour mark came, the chances were coming thick and fast. Too fast for my liking. Call me superstitious, but I started to wonder if this was going to be our night. I must've seen a hundred games like this one over the years. It was beginning to look like one of those matches when we had all the chances, only for their keeper to play a blinder and keep us out.

Pretty soon they'd dropped so deep, even their front two were on the edge of their own box. They'd obviously come here to hold onto their slender lead from the first leg and spoil our magnificent football with a load of cynical time-wasting.

Alexander-Arnold continued to terrorise them out wide, peppering the box with crosses which had them struggling to clear their lines. Then, just before half-time, we got our just rewards. Another cross, this time from the bye-line, this time from the right boot of Oxlade-Chamberlain. This time the Dutchmen didn't miss. A downward header beat the keeper and found the back of the net. Just like last year's semi-final, *Gini* had scored.

The Kop exploded. Fists were pumped, red flags were waved and some hooligans even let off a couple of flares. We'd levelled the match, so they'd have to come out and play us in the second half. If they'd only move the team bus from in front of the goal, I fancied our chances here. We could probably win this one by a cricket score.

A moment later, the ref blew his whistle and we went into the break all square. We sang and danced right through the interval, awaiting our boys to return to finish the job. We had their knackers on the chopping block now, all we had to do was strike.

When the second-half came, it was one-way traffic. Salah broke down the right but couldn't quite wrap his foot around the ball to put us ahead. Another low drive from Oxlade-Chamberlain fizzed off the keeper's palms, but this time it went behind for a corner. It seemed only a matter of time now.

Alexander-Arnold's free-kick found Firmino at the back post, but the keeper was there to make the stop. Next it was the crossbar's turn to deny a Robertson header and I started to wonder how much more I could take.

Alexander-Arnold whipped in a corner which caused chaos in the box, but in the end a defender lumped it clear. A minute later he cracked another one at goal from all of thirty yards, which was still too hot for their keeper to handle. This time the rebound went our way, falling to Robertson, but his shot was blocked by Trippier. We were all over them now.

Oxlade-Chamberlain surged down the right. Mane down the left. We were killing them with width. Corner after corner. Some pumped into the box, only to be headed away. Others were well-worked short balls, one of which teed up a lovely chance for Robertson. For a moment I thought we'd finally picked the lock, only to have my hopes dashed as he blasted his effort over the bar.

Ten minutes from time and Klopp brought on the *auld* man, much to the delight of the Kop who started singing, 'There's only one Jamie Milner.' By now, we'd thrown everything but my Nan's knickers at them and still the scores were tied. With extra-time looming, there was plenty of football left in this one, but I couldn't help but think Madrid were already holding out for penalties. They probably had been since half-time.

Milner had an immediate impact, crossing from the left to find Wijnaldum. *Gini* headed it back across the goal to Mane, who attempted the most sublime overhead kick which narrowly missed the target. Maybe on another night that would've gone in.

After a quick break for water, we went into extra-time. Thankfully, the *Flying Dutchman* came out firing, although this time our scorer turned provider. Nothing was straightforward that night and, when Wijnaldum's cross found Firmino at the back post, the woodwork denied his first attempt. But the ball rebounded our way, *Bobby* banged it into the back of the net and put us twenty-five minutes away from another Champions League final.

We were dancing and singing so loud, it was almost like a tsunami. If this was a work of fiction, I would finish off by telling you how we added a couple more and it all ended there, with a few beers down the *Willow* afterwards for good measure. But it didn't. A few minutes later Adrián scuffed an easy clearance into the path of Felix, who played a finely weighted ball on for Llorente. I couldn't watch what happened next, but when I opened my eyes our keeper was picking the ball out of his own net. It was probably the first time they'd crossed the halfway line for over an hour and they'd only gone and *purra flukes gob on us.*

Even though the scores were tied, with the dreaded away goals rule, we needed another now. Henderson chipped one forward for Salah, but his sweetly struck volley went over the bar. We had no choice but to throw bodies forward. That's what allowed Llorente in for another. He struck a clean effort just on the edge of the box, whilst Milner and Henderson watched on, unable to close him down. Somehow, despite all the possession and chances, we found ourselves two behind now. On came Origi, Fabinho and Minamio. Once again we pushed forward. Mane looked the biggest threat, driving the ball across their six-yard box only for the keeper to push it away. A minute later he was fouled in the box, but there was nothing doing from the ref. The footballing gods weren't smiling on us that night. Our heads dropped, not just on the pitch, but in the stands too. In the end, Marata added insult to injury with a last minute drive at Adrián's near post and we crashed out of the Champions League four-two on aggregate.

I must've been the last one to leave the ground, left amongst the losing betting slips and empty pie-trays. Worst of all, I didn't know where to put myself. I wasn't lying when I said Anfield was the place I felt closest to Kenny. But truth be told, I heard his voice everywhere, from the pub, to the betting shop. And sometimes, it all got too much. By now, I already realised tonight was going to be one of those nights. Kenny was already in my ear, whispering away, 'If you ask me it's fucking Klopp's fault for throwing too many bodies forward. I never liked that *Gerry* bastard, anyway.'

And I thought I was out of touch. Some days he sounded more *antwacky* than Stan Boardman. Still, I couldn't blame him, he had been dead for over thirty years. As I eventually left the stadium, I already knew what I was going to do. I was going to get absolutely fucking bladdered. I wasn't daft, I knew it wouldn't shut Kenny up altogether, but it might just tone him down a little. At least that's what I said at the countless meetings I'd been to over the years. If it wasn't true, then it was a lie I'd told myself often enough, I'd started to believe it.

I checked my pockets. There wasn't even enough coppers to buy a pint in the Willow, let alone a round, which was probably for the best. There were a couple of *meffs* I didn't want to bump into down there. So it was going to be the last of those little bottles of wine the Doctor had prescribed me. If I mixed them up right, I could probably make myself a *red biddy*. That's when I heard ar Kenny again, scratching away in my ear. 'What is it our arl Fella used to say?' he mumbled, as I staggered down the street on my *Rob Jones*. 'Life's a shit

25

sandwich, but the more bread you've got, the less shit you have to taste.'

I laughed so hard, I actually cried. After all, you can't deny ar arl Fella did seem to swear an awful lot for a Lutheran Minister. But at least one of those tears was for ar Richie, even though he *jibbed* me off earlier. He'd have loved that one.

Chapter 3
Richie Kennedy
11th March 2020

With that nasty business with ar Wayne still whirling around my head like an action replay, I was pretty relieved to see a friendly face as I rolled into the car park. Even though she was nearly thirty, I still couldn't get over how grown-up ar Lauren looked these days, or *Lozzle* as we called her. Despite the fact I didn't see her nearly as often as I should, I thought of her more like a daughter than a sister. She wasn't even born when ar Kenny died and I suppose that made it easier for her. In all honesty, she was probably the *auld* folk's attempt at starting again, not that I would ever say it to her face. With the massive age difference, both Wayne and I did our best to spoil her growing up, although we probably made her teenage years a total nightmare being a bit overprotective. God help any boys she tried to bring home, it's like she had three arl Fellas to scare them off.

'Nice set of wheels,' she said, as the *Tesla* reversed itself into a charging bay. 'Where's Wayne?'

'Don't ask,' I replied, throwing my arms around her as I got out. 'But it's great to see you.'

'Oh, that bad,' she tutted. 'It didn't come to blows did it?'

27

'Not quite,' I replied. 'He wanted to go to the footy, that's all. Can you believe it? Today of all days.'

'He probably just wanted to hang out with you.' She always did this, played referee to our arguments. Although trust me, she knew how to issue a yellow card if either of us overstepped the mark. 'At least he came down to London to see you.'

'Only because Ma made him,' I said. 'And to be fair, he stunk of booze. Although I might have made that situation worse.'

'You didn't offer him a drink, did you?' Lozzle said, scornfully. 'For fuck sake Richie, he's got an illness.'

'It was only one,' I said. 'We went to Kenny's memorial and I was trying to bond with him or something.'

'Men!' Lozzle exclaimed, shaking her head with disbelief. 'Why couldn't you just tell him you missed him.'

'I did,' I replied, desperate to change the subject already. 'How are you anyway? How's the boyfriend?'

Lozzle rolled her eyes in mock-horror. 'He has a name you know.'

'Sorry, how's Giles…the blue nose?' I added, unable to resist.

'Oh for fuck sake, there's more to life than what football team you support,' Lozzle snapped.

'That's exactly what I said to ar Wayne.' I said.

'I'm not doing it.' She smiled, just to let me know she wasn't really angry. 'I know what you're trying to do and I'm not doing it.'

'Doing what?' I asked, as if I didn't know what she was getting at.

'Taking sides,' she said, grabbing hold of my arm. 'Now come on, let's go see the arl Fella.'

As we made our way to the main entrance, I couldn't get over the stark contrast from the streets outside. It was absolutely desolate, like a scene from some zombie apocalypse movie. A tired-looking nurse stopped us at the door and asked ar Lozzle why she was here. I wondered if they knew each other at first, but it turned out ar Lozzle had been off for a week on compassionate leave and she was a little bit out of the loop. Whilst the nurse let us in, she warned us they were waiting on an announcement next week and pretty soon it would be emergency visits only.

I'm sure nobody likes the *ozzy*, but the emptiness only made things worse. The sound of our footsteps filled me with terror as we trudged up the main corridor. I was glad to have ar Lozzle for company, I'd have never found the way on my own. One long corridor after another, followed by a number of lefts and rights, but eventually we arrived safely at the stroke ward. It was a horrible place if I'm honest, beds poking out from behind curtains, which were so miserable they must've been specially designed for unconscious people. The sound of ventilators rising up and down filled the air, occasionally interrupted by the beep of heart-rate monitors.

In the last bay by the window was my arl Fella. It wasn't a pretty sight, his feet poking out the end of the bed like two mouldy lumps of stilton and my Ma sat beside him, fluffing up his pillow. 'Richie!' she said, making a beeline straight for us. 'I wasn't expecting you until the morning.'

'Really?' I said, a little overwhelmed with all the attention. 'I thought you knew I was coming up tonight.'

'Yeah, but I thought you might've gone to the footy with your brother,' she said.

'With the arl Fella like that?' I swallowed hard. It was difficult to imagine this was the giant man who used to carry me around on his shoulders, tubes coming out of his mouth and his face like *punctured custard*. But at least his eyes were closed. That's what I'd found most difficult to endure through all these years. It was like a certain light had gone out on that day when Kenny passed away. Not that you'd have noticed, if you didn't know him like I did. He was made out of stern stuff ar arl Fella. His father had been a boat builder in Belfast and his grandfather a steel worker from

30

Motherwell. You could say he came from a long line of proper hard men.

That's why it always seemed strange, his choice of profession. Not that he ever pushed God or Jesus on any of us growing up. He wasn't that kind of preacher. He enjoyed a drink, he smoked like a trooper and he swore like one too. He wasn't a violent man, but let's just say if you were going to have a ruck, you'd have wanted him on your team. He just had this way of fixing people, that's all. Apart from us lot. Nobody could fix ar family of fuck-ups.

'It's not like Ezzy is going anywhere soon,' Ma said, dabbing at the arl Fella's brow with a cloth. 'Not for a few days anyway.'

By now Lozzle was stood at the foot of the bed, rifling through his notes. 'Test results look really good,' she said. 'According to this his surgery went really well.'

'That's what the consultant said this afternoon,' Ma replied. 'Apparently he's just very tired and weak, so they've put him into a coma to help him rest. They plan to wake him up in the next couple of days, or by the weekend at the very latest. You will still be here won't you Richie? I know you have to work, but I'm sure he'd love to see you.'

'Of course,' I replied. 'I'm booked in for at least a couple of weeks.'

'Booked in?' Ma glared at me and I couldn't quite make out whether she was confused or disappointed. 'I thought you were staying with us. I made a bed up for you in Kenny's *auld* room.'

'No,' I replied, not quite able to hold her stare. 'I'm staying at the *Plaza.* I was worried some *blert* might mess with my motor outside ours.' I knew it was a mistake the moment I said it. Ma had kept Kenny's room like a shrine and here I was wittering on about my car. Although, to be honest, I had other reasons. I just didn't want to go into them right now.

Lozzle kicked me sharply under the bed, before coming to my rescue. 'I think what Richie means is he's got a lot of work to do and he wouldn't want to disturb us on the phone at all hours.'

'You wouldn't disturb me,' Ma said, pointing at a crumpled pile of blankets wedged against the back of the chair she'd been sitting on. 'And Lozzle's still off at the moment. It would just be nice to have all my children under one roof for a change. I could even get ar Wayne round for Sunday lunch if everything goes to plan.'

'You can't sleep here,' I said, desperately trying to change the subject. 'You've got to keep your strength up for when the *auld* man wakes up.'

'I'll be fine,' Ma replied, turning to *Lozzle*. 'Which reminds me, any chance you can pop over tomorrow and give Wayne's flat the once over? You know I usually do it, but I've been tied up here with Ezzy all week.'

'If I have to,' Lozzle replied, pulling a face like a smacked arse. 'But you can't keep mothering him like that. I'm not sure it's really helping him in the long run.'

We both knew she was wasting her breath. Ma might've been a bit behind the times when it came to women's rights, but she was like a proper *Mother Treesa* when it came to us three. Although God help anyone from outside who crossed one of us.

Talking idly across the arl Fella's bed, we must have sat there until gone ten o'clock. Once I got over the initial shock of how frail he looked, I almost became accustomed to looking at him. I suppose he appeared kind of peaceful really, like he was fast asleep and free from life's worries. Still, I couldn't help but wonder if Ma was being a bit over optimistic with her plans for Sunday lunch.

I considered asking ar Lozzle about it on the way home, seeing as she was a nurse and everything, but I thought better of it in the end. I wasn't ready for the truth if it turned out to be bad news, not with everything else going on in London.

So instead I tuned the radio into *Five Live*, hoping to catch the end of the *footy*.

The streets seemed half-empty by the time we made it to *Tockie*, so I already suspected we might've failed to overturn the one goal deficit from the first leg, but I was shocked to hear they'd stuck three past us and actually beaten us at Anfield. That was it, less than a year had passed and we were no longer Champions of Europe. 'Wayne's gonna have a proper sore head in the morning,' I said, turning to ar Lozzle

'At least you haven't got to clean his pigsty of a flat,' Lozzle replied.

'Well, let me make it up to you,' I said. 'Meet me for lunch at the *Plaza* when you're done.'

'Oh go on then,' she giggled, as we pulled up outside the house where I grew up. 'But honestly, what's this about some *blert* messing with your car if you stayed round here? I don't want to sound like Wayne, but you can be a right whacker sometimes.'

'It's not that,' I said, feeling my bottom lip start to tremble. 'I suppose you'll find out sooner or later. I'm getting a divorce.'

'Oh, Richie,' Lozzle said, throwing her arms around me. 'I am sorry, but I can't say I'm surprised.'

'Forty-five years old and I just didn't want to move back in with my parents,' I said, not even thinking how insensitive that might've sounded to ar Lozzle, who worked damn hard and still lived at home whilst she was saving for her own place. Instead, I just broke down. Tears started streaming down my face, but they weren't exactly tears of sadness.

Truthfully, I wasn't that bothered about the divorce, my marriage had pretty much ended before it began. Of course, I was upset at seeing the arl Fella and Ma like that and I really regretted that awful business with Wayne earlier. But to be honest, I think part of me was still crying for ar Kenny. After all these years, his passing still weighed heavily on all of us. We still hadn't found peace or justice. Not a single one of us. I think those tears were just a massive release.

Chapter 4

Lauren Kennedy

11th March 2020

By the time I got through the door I was absolutely shattered. I'd only been off work for a week and I was already dreading going back. Not only was this coronavirus situation getting far more serious, but it was our ward in the ICU which was inevitably going to bear the brunt of it. Throw Ma, the arl Fella and my bloody brothers into the mix and I already knew it was a recipe for a nervous breakdown. They all assumed because I wasn't born when Kenny passed away, that somehow, it hadn't affected me. Which was utter bollocks. Kenny's ghost had haunted ar family for over thirty years, me included. Even when they weren't talking about him, they were avoiding talking about him, if you know what I mean.

The fall-out was written all over their faces, every minute, of every day. So it was no surprise I invented this imaginary friend called *Kenny the Clown* when I was a kid. Looking back, it was probably pretty upsetting for my *auld* folks, although other than ar Wayne, nobody seemed to pay a sprat of notice. Except on this one morning. The morning of my fifth birthday, when I drew a picture of him in a red shirt, with black circles under his eyes and his face all white and puffy. I'll never forget it. Apparently, I came running down the *rattlers* and asked my arl folks if Kenny the clown was coming to my party. I didn't mean to make my *auld* Ma cry, but it did piss on my Nan's trifle.

My eyelids already felt heavy as I took off my makeup and got myself ready for bed. It's only when I went to set my alarm that I noticed a number of missed calls. It was nearly eleven o'clock by then, but I assumed he'd still be awake.

'Hey, babes. It's only me,' I said, safely wrapped under the duvet, when Giles finally picked up. 'Sorry it's so late. I've just got back from seeing my arl Fella again.'

'How is he?' Giles asked.

'No better,' I said. 'But I don't think he's suffering.'

'Well, that's at least something,' Giles replied. 'Look, I was wondering what you were up to Saturday?'

'Saturday?' I said, finding it hard to think that far ahead. 'Not a lot. I might go and visit the arl Fella again. If I'm not called back to work early.'

'Have a day off,' Giles said. 'I know it's serious, but things are bound to be tougher than usual when you go back and you need to think of yourself occasionally.'

I couldn't deny he had a point. 'So where are you taking us then?'

'Well, don't say no before you think about it,' Giles said, teasing me as always. He was a hopeless romantic that one.

'Don't worry, you had me the moment I found out your arl Fella was loaded,' I teased.

'Great, well it's the Merseyside derby at Goodison Park on Saturday and...'

'No chance,' I said, interrupting him. 'My brothers would kill me. And you for that matter.'

'I know. You're a red and I'm a blue, but my parents are coming over and I would really like to introduce you.'

'I don't know.'

'Come on, it'll be like the Montagues and the Capulets,' he said, the smooth talking bastard. 'I'll be Romeo and you can be Juliet.'

'What's wrong with watching it at their gaff on the Wirral?' I protested.

'It's complicated, Lozzle,' he said, knowing full well I loved it when he called me that. 'Come on, be a sport.'

'Alright, but I'm wearing red,' I replied.

'So, does that mean you're coming then?' Giles asked.

'It's a date,' I said, reluctantly. 'But I've got to sleep now. You've no idea what I've signed myself up for tomorrow.'

'Worse than the Merseyside derby?' he asked.

'Much worse!'

I was still in my dressing gown when a horn started blaring outside. It must've been Ma who'd booked the taxi, the note saying *thank you* and the two carrier bags on the kitchen table were the giveaway. One was filled with chicken soup and the other with bottles of bleach and disinfectant. Who knows when she'd found time to buy them, let alone pop back and put them there, but somebody really ought to tell her it was over a hundred years since Emily Wilding-Davison leapt in front of the King's horse. Why the heck she expected me to clean my older brother's flat was beyond me. He was almost fifty for fuck's sake.

Shoving on an old scruffy sweater, a pair of leggings and my boss new *trabs*, I hurried outside and apologised to the poor driver for keeping him waiting. He must have thought I was a right *meff*. Although, he never let on. He was one of those chatty-cabbies, who kept going on about last night's football. He couldn't believe it when I told him I couldn't care less. I know I'd made a fuss about wearing red to the Merseyside derby with Giles, but I was only teasing him. With his well-paid job, working for his arl Fella, I knew ar Giles was far too good for me really. Football was the only thing I had over him. Liverpool were much better than Everton. I'm not saying it because my whole family supported them, it was just a fact. Still, I couldn't fathom why the players got paid so much or why they had so many different competitions. The Premier League, the Europa League, the Champions League, the League Cup, the FA Cup, the World Cup. Sometimes I wondered why they didn't all just play once, decide who was the best and leave it at that.

By the time I arrived, I wished I hadn't bothered coming so early. Ar Wayne was still in his underpants when he finally answered the door, off-white belly warmers, with piss stains up the middle. At least I hoped that's what they were. 'Come here Lozzle, give your big brother a hug why don't you?' he said.

To be honest, I thought it might be bleeding obvious, seeing as he smelt like a wrestler's armpit, but I couldn't bring myself to tell him. 'I can't Wayne, we've all been warned at work to try and keep ar distance,' I said convincingly, even though I hadn't been to work for over a week now.

As I stepped inside the door, I almost gagged. You couldn't actually see the floor, instead there was a carpet of pizza boxes, porno mags and beer cans. 'I know, it looks like a *bombsitted* in here,' he said, sheepishly.

Like always, I had no idea what he was on about but, *oh my god, what a fucking shit-hole* and Ma wondered why I

41

didn't want to introduce him to Giles. It hadn't helped that he'd flown off the handle and refused to speak to me for a week after he found out Giles supported Everton.

'You know I used to think it was all one word. He grinned, revealing a big gap where his front teeth used to be. Just for a second, I felt a tiny bit sorry for him. 'I was your age before I realised Ma was actually saying *like a bomb has hit it.*'

'Talking of Ma, she bought you these,' I said, dropping both bags off into the kitchen and turning round to make a run for it. What I really wanted was to go to town and buy a new coat before I visited Richie at the *Plaza*. A good coat coupled with some decent shoes always covered a multitude of sins, including the Liverpool shirt I intended on wearing on my date with Giles at the weekend.

'Be a darl and put the kettle on then,' he said, seemingly oblivious to my body language. God only knows why, but I did. Followed by picking up the crap from the living room floor and giving it a once over with the hoover. I don't know how *Henry* remained so bloody happy. I'm not sure I could've smiled my way through sucking up all that shit off the floor. Still, it was nothing compared to what was waiting for me in the *clossit*. After fumbling around with my thumb and forefinger clamped over my nostrils, I eventually managed to flush it down. Then I crouched down and got to work with a knackered old bog brush which I found beside the pan. To be honest, I was tempted to use ar Wayne's toothbrush just to teach him a lesson.

'Sorry about that,' he said, patting me on the shoulder, as I scrubbed away, furiously. 'I've had the *Bombay Crud* of late.'

I knew he meant well, but I couldn't help but feel like a dirty tart who had just knelt down to perform the unmentionable. 'How did things go with Richie?' I asked, knowing it was a mistake, but I had to do something to get the unspeakable image out of my head.

'That little whacker. Can you believe he ended up needing a sat-nav to find his way to Toxteth Cemetery.'

'I'm sure that's not true,' I said, realising I was coming dangerously close to taking sides. 'I'm going over to see him later, maybe I'll talk to him.'

'Great, maybe I'll tag along,' he replied. 'He might listen if we both told him what a whacker he's become.'

By now I was starting to wish I hadn't mentioned it. *Think Lauren, think.* I know it sounds horrible, but I couldn't imagine walking into the Plaza with ar Wayne on my arm. I certainly didn't want to end up refereeing another one of their rows. 'Are you sure you're feeling up to it?'

43

'To be honest, me and Richie are never going to get along,' he said. 'Besides, you two don't want me cramping your style.'

'It's not that Wayne, it's just with this virus lurking about and your immune system being weakened by your...' I paused, trying to find a polite word for *lazyitis*.

'You're right,' he agreed. 'Where would I be without you?'

Dead in an alleyway, I thought, standing up to admire my own handy work. 'It's not your fault, you're unwell, that's all.'

'True enough,' he said. 'But I don't suppose you'd nip down the baggy for me.'

'The what?' I asked.

'I've got some clothes that need washing.'

'Oh sure, just give them here.' I said, realising it was my chance to make a swift getaway.

A few loud bangs later and he came back wearing a loose-fitting dressing gown, holding a stack of dirty clothes. None of it was folded, instead it was hanging out the top of one of those plaid nylon bags, with the zips that always break. The ones homeless people use to carry all their shit around town. Thank god the laundrette was just around the corner, I was going to look like a right *meff* lugging that about. 'Oh and I almost forgot,' he said, disappearing back into his room. There were a couple more loud bangs before he emerged with a battered *auld* shoe box. 'If you see the arl Fella, can you give him these?'

I was surprised to find it full of faded photographs. Pictures of him playing football with Kenny. There were even a couple of Richie and a lovely one of the *auld* folks before they got married. They looked so young and happy. 'You should give them to him yourself,' I said. 'To be honest, he's not awake at the moment, but I'm sure Ma would love to see you.'

'You're right, Lozzle. And I really would,' he said, pausing for a moment. 'But I'm just in a spot of bother at the moment.'

By now I felt really sorry for him, but somebody had to say it. 'Listen Wayne, you're not the only one with a spot of bother on at the moment. I'm not going to lie to you, I'm not sure the arl Fella is going to pull through this one. Not with this dreaded virus kicking about.'

'Of course he will,' Wayne said, but I could see it in his eyes that I'd rattled him. 'Oh and one more thing before you go.' He went back into his room and came out holding what looked like a dead dog wrapped in brown paper. I say wrapped in the loosest possible sense, whatever he was

45

holding was already sealed in cellophane and he'd kind of taped a paper bag to the top of it. 'For you, I can't have you meeting up with this new fella of yours looking like a complete *meff*, can I?'

'Really?' I said, surprised at how understanding he was being. But not half as surprised as I was when I finally got inside the cellophane wrapper. 'A Louis Vuitton coat. Is it real?'

'Of course it's real,' he scowled. 'I had a bit of luck on the *gee-gees.*'

It was proper *stoosh*. Now it was me leaning in for a hug and ar Wayne stepping back. In the confusion, one of us must have trodden on the *auld* box of photographs. That's when I saw it, staring back at me. 'Oh my god, is that my drawing of Kenny the clown?'

Wayne just shrugged his shoulders, looking pretty miffed by it all. 'I guess so. Have it if you want, I didn't even know it was in there.'

I picked it up and held it close to my chest. Then with my other hand, as if Kenny the clown was urging me on, I pushed Wayne all the way back into the bathroom and shut the door behind him. 'Come on, get yourself cleaned up and we'll go and see Richie together. I'm not taking no for an answer.'

Chapter 5
Richie Kennedy
12th March 2020

It was eleven o'clock when I eventually got off the phone. Apparently, Mags' solicitors had finally agreed to the terms. About bloody time, if you asked me. It reminded me of a client's case a few years back, which ended up being a career defining moment, for him at least, not me. By the time her legal team were done, his ex-wife was not only entitled to half of everything he made during their marriage, she was also due a hefty wedge of his future earnings too. I remember him saying how his newborn child, with his supermodel girlfriend, would still be paying the price long after he passed away. Well, I hadn't even got any kids, let alone a supermodel girlfriend, and my great grandchildren would be footing the bill for this one.

I was pretty sure I'd have to sell my apartment in London, which was on the eleventh floor of a shiny skyscraper overlooking the South Bank of the Thames. It was my own fault for sticking her name on the mortgage. Truth be told, she hadn't put a penny of her own money into the pot, it just helped us get a lower rate of interest. By now I was proper down the banks and it was still a couple hours before I'd agreed to meet ar Lozzle. So I decided to take a soothing drive in my new car. At least I'd had the sense to purchase that through the company. With its zero emissions, not only did I get a huge tax break, it was safe from the clutches of Mags' money grabbing solicitors.

I thought about going back to the cemetery in *Tockie*, but I couldn't quite face it. So I swerved that and went down the docks to clear my head. That's where I first saw her. She was coming out of JD Sports, wearing a tight, black vest and a baggy pair of football shorts. I knew I'd been under pressure lately, but this Judy was unmistakable. Melanie Andrews. How could I forget? She looked like Sinita but spoke like Carol Decker. Which made her both posh and exotic if you came from round ar way. Everybody wanted to shag her at school, but she only had eyes for ar Kenny. I'm not surprised, he was a good-looking bastard and one hell of a centre-forward. He could pretty much take his pick when it came to the gerls. Before I thought about how sleazy it must've looked, I'd stuck the car into self-drive and wound down the window to talk to her. 'Hey, Mel, is that you? You look unbelievable!'

She looked up and replied in a scouse accent, which I suddenly realised sounded far more authentic than mine.

'Sheil Road is that way, luv. Go back after dark and you might even get a freebie driving that thing.'

'Don't be like that Melanie, it's Richie. Ken's brother.'

She picked up the pace, obviously trying to lose me as we approached a pedestrian crossing. 'I don't know a Melanie, or a Ken for that matter.'

That's when I realised, it couldn't be her. She hadn't aged a day. 'Sorry luv, you just look so much like a *Judy* I used to know at school. Melanie Andrews.'

'Do you mean Melody Andrews?' she replied, looking a little more friendly now.

Ar shit, how could I have got that one wrong? Maybe ar Kenny was right, maybe I had become a total whacker. 'I beg your pardon, do you know her?'

'Know her?' she replied. 'She was my bloody mother.'

'Was?' I said, with a lump in my throat. 'What do you mean, *was*?'

'She passed away about thirty years ago, giving birth to me.'

I started to do the maths. Despite my disastrous divorce settlement, which seemed to suggest otherwise, I always had been good with numbers. 'Fuck me, you don't look old enough.'

49

'You're a right bloody charmer, you are,' she said, slowing down to a standstill.

I shifted the car into park and stuck my hazard lights on. 'Look, I know how dodgy this sounds, but can I buy you a coffee? It's just my brother Ken used to date your Ma back in high school.'

She leant into my open window and flexed one of her giant biceps, just to let me know she'd totally kick my arse if I tried anything. 'Go on then,' she said. 'I've got about an hour before practice.'

I found a safe spot to park the car and met her at the *Starbucks* round the corner. I won't lie, it felt awkward as hell, considering I was nearly old enough to be her arl Fella and I'd just picked her up on the side of the street. 'I don't usually use my car to chat-up *gerls*, I promise.'

'Why not? It's a damn sight better looking than you,' she joked, before ordering a large latte and a stack of pastries. She probably thought I was good for the money. Not that I minded, I just wondered where she planned on sticking them all. 'Is it a Tesla?'

'That's right, a Performance Model 3,' I said, realising how geeky I must've sounded, but desperate to fill the uncomfortable silence with some form of conversation. 'Sorry, I didn't catch your name.'

'Amber,' she replied. 'So do you want to tell me what my Ma was like at school? Is that why you stopped me?'

'If you like,' I said, sipping at my coffee. 'Well, I guess we've already established she looked a lot like you, only a little less sporty. In fact, she used to dress like one of the Bangles.'

'Oh my god, I love that song,' she said, excitedly.

'Which one?' I asked. "Please don't say *Eternal Flame*.'

'Nah, *Manic Monday*, I'm always running late, me!' she said, slurping the milky foam from the top of her cup and somehow making me feel a lot less self-conscious in the process. 'Anyway, I don't always dress like this, it's just I've got footy practice in an hour and I needed some new boots.'

'Where do you play?'

'Merseyrail Ladies on Admiral Street.'

'No,' I said, smiling. 'What position do you play?'

'Centre forward,' she said, flexing her muscles again. 'Can't you tell?'

There was so much I wanted to ask her, but in the end I just nodded and said, 'Like me brother Ken.'

'He was one of my Ma's boyfriends at school, right?'

Come on Richie, you need to tread very carefully here.

'You could say that,' I replied, lying through my teeth. I didn't want to push it any further, but Kenny was her *only* boyfriend at school. And although she was the spitting image of her Ma, there was something about the shape of her eyes which reminded me of ar Kenny now too. 'She was very popular at school.'

'So I've heard,' she replied, and I wondered what she was getting at.

Amber turned out to be a right *laff* and one cup of coffee soon became two. In fact, she kept me talking so long, I had to give her a lift across town, so she didn't miss her training session. Still, she insisted on getting out at the top of Admiral Road, saying she could use the half-mile run as a warm-up.

'Can I have your number?' I asked, leaning out the window as she left. 'I'd love to come and watch your next match.'

'Okay, it's tomorrow at the Recreational Ground if you're genuinely interested,' she said, snatching the phone out of my hand and punching in her digits. 'If it doesn't get cancelled for Coronavirus.'

'Maybe I'll see you tomorrow then?' I asked, amazed how quickly things were developing and the speed in which her thumbs moved across my screen.

'I'd like that,' she said. Then she pecked me on the cheek, before dropping my phone deliberately into my lap.

It almost felt as if I'd been slapped across the face, as she jogged off down the street. Of course I didn't want to read too much into that kiss, seeing as she might be my long-lost niece and all, but I'd never really understood the subtle meaning of these things. It dated back to school. The *gerls* used to swarm around ar Kenny, even ar Wayne for that matter. Whereas I was always nervous. The geeky one. I suppose it was a bit like the offside rule. Whilst I had no problem there, I was often amazed how some people could never seem to grasp it. Well, women were my offside rule. It didn't matter how many sauce bottles you spread across the dinner table, or how many times you explained it, I was never going to understand them.

Still, it was nothing compared to the confusion I felt when I finally returned to the *Plaza.* I nearly spilt my guts when ar Lozzle rocked up with ar Wayne in tow. Not only had the arl *meff* had the cheek to show his face, he even looked good. She'd obviously helped him get dressed. He was clean-shaven, wearing a navy blue blazer, which had a Liverpool handker*chief* poking out of the lapel pocket. She'd even got him to stick his front teeth in. 'Hey,' I said, not quite able to look my brother in the eye, after *ar* little spat yesterday. 'I see you both made it in the end then.'

Wayne appeared not to notice, either that or not to care. 'You alright, Rich?'

'I'm good,' I replied, holding out my hand like an olive branch. 'You?'

'Living the bloody dream, *La*,' he replied, leaving me hanging for a moment, before almost breaking my wrist with a bone-crushing handshake. He always did have the arl Fella's strength.

We sat down and ordered a round of drinks. I had a pint of Carlsberg and so did Lozzle. I love a *Judy* who can sink a proper *bevvie*. Although much to my surprise, ar Wayne only had sparkling water. 'Don't worry my *arl meff*, I'm getting these, so tuck in,' I said, realising a little too late that I'd only gone and offered him a drink again.

'You bloody well aren't,' Wayne replied. 'And don't you arl *meff* me.'

'Don't start,' Lozzle interrupted. 'I'll get them in. After all, look at the *boss* new coat ar Wayne got us.'

'Really?' I said, noticing the designer label on her lapel. Even though she was my sister and she was only wearing a pair of leggings and a sweatshirt beneath that coat, she was a total knock-out ar Lozzle.

'When have we actually ever done this anyway?' she asked.

'Done what?' I replied, unsure of what she was getting at.

'The three of us, sat down and had a meal together, without Ma or the arl Fella,' she exclaimed.

'Oh come on, we must've done it sometime,' Wayne said, sipping nervously at his water.

'If we have, then I can't think when,' I added.

'I take it you went to see the arl Fella?' Wayne asked, and I wondered if he was going to start again.

'Yep, although you didn't miss much,' I said, trying to keep the peace. 'He's still completely out of it.'

There was another long pause before ar Lozzle cut in. 'Don't get down the banks. It's early days, but provided he doesn't catch that bloody virus, then he might pull through this one yet.' I loved the way she ended up sounding more *antwacky* with every second she spent with us.

'He's got to,' Wayne said. 'I still owe him a tenner.'

'A bit more than a tenner,' I added. Whilst I didn't want a row, it had to be said. Over the years, he'd pretty much rinsed the *auld* folks dry.

'What did I tell you two?' Lozzle said, pulling out a piece of paper from her purse and lying it flat across the table. 'Now, look what I found at Wayne's earlier.'

And there it was, from ar Lozzle's infamous fifth birthday party. 'Is that what I think it is?'

'Yep,' she said, as if she was completely unaware of how much trouble it had caused. 'It's Kenny the clown.'

Now, if I couldn't remember us ever sitting down for a meal without my arl folks, I definitely couldn't remember us openly talking about ar Kenny together. 'You'll never guess what happened to me,' I said, finally plucking up the courage to mention it. 'Although I'm sure you'll both think I'm crazy.'

'Go on,' Wayne said. 'You, finally admitting to being crazy. This'll be good.'

And I was just about to tell them how I might have discovered *ar* long-lost niece, when the waiter arrived to take our order. 'I'll tell you later, let's have a good time first.'

Chapter 6
Wayne Kennedy
13th March 2020

For the first time in years, I woke up sober. Despite the achievement, it was a bit overrated to be honest. I was spitting like a *Flemish comedian* and my gob tasted like the bottom of a *berdcage*. Don't get me wrong, I had an absolute belter at the *cokes* last night, even though I didn't have so much as a sniff of the barmaid's apron, but now I was *moodying* about, looking for *Harry Freeman's* to go with *me bur de goo*. I was literally minding my own business when who should start up, but *ar kid*, Kenny. It's not that I didn't want to hear from him, it's just I didn't want to hear from him that early in the morning. '*Boogeroff*, Ken or I'll fucking *marmalise yer*.'

'That's charming that is,' Kenny said. 'Now you're back to being *bezzies* with that *whacker* Richie, you don't wanna *knows* us anymore.'

'Don't get *airyated*.' I said. 'I just want to go and see ar arl Fella today, that's all.'

'So that's it then?' Kenny said. 'Here's your hat and where's the hurry?'

'*Come 'ed* if you must.' I sighed.

'*Swerve* that,' he said. 'Neither of us can go down the *ozzy* today.'

'Why's that?' I asked.

'For a start it's Friday the thirteenth.'

'Give over.' I replied. 'I don't believe in that shite.'

'Secondly, it's the first day of Cheltenham,' he said and suddenly he had my attention.

'Ken, how many times do I have to tell you?' I begged, trying to jib him off. 'I'm done with all that shit.'

'Come on,' he continued. 'You know I struggle to look into the arl Fella's eyes at the best of times. And if I'm not wrong, you still owe the *Deli Mob* ten bags, don't you?'

'Twenty,' I said. 'But who's counting.'

'So, let's go down the *Willow* and sink a couple of *bevvies* and I'll let you know which of the *nags* are coming in this afternoon. You'll make enough to square away the *latch-lifter* and then we'll both go and see the arl Fella this evening, like a couple of winners.'

'I don't know, Ken. You've been proper off of late.'

'Bollocks, look at that stoosh coat I helped you get for ar Lozzle,' he said and I couldn't deny he had a point.

'Alright,' I said. 'But I ain't sinking a single lush.'

'We'll see about that, my arl *meff*,' Kenny replied. 'We'll see!'

So off I went, bowling into the *Willow* with every intention of ordering a glass of water at the bar, but when I opened my mouth it was like ar Kenny took over. A *black and tan* with a *Pope's phone number* on the side. Then of course, I had to get him one back, otherwise he'd only get onto me saying, 'Where were you when I had all the coppers.'

So by the time we got to the bookies, I wasn't exactly *parlatic,* but my legs was jangling a bit. So were my nerves. There were a couple of *blert*s loitering by the door, which I didn't like the look of. I don't think they were Deli Mob, otherwise they'd have definitely hung one on us, but still they made me feel uneasy. 'Takes a man not a shirt button,' ar Ken said, as they headed back onto the street.

'Leave it out,' I said, taking myself over to the corner to study the *Racing Post*. 'You'd start a row in an empty house, you.'

'So have you got the splosh?' Kenny asked, as brazen as a brass nail.

'I might have a bob or two.' I said, still a bit unsure about all of this.

'Right then. Go and stick it all on *Harry Trotter* in the first,' he laughed. 'On the nose.'

I nearly did for a second. 'Wait a minute, *Harry Trotter*? You must think I was born yesterday.'

'Just testing you, my arl *meff*.' Kenny always did this. Pissed me about and pulled my pants down. 'You're going to want *Burning Victory* in the one-thirty, and if you hold your horses, he should go off at twelve to one.'

'Are you sure? I can't see him getting past the favourite, *Goshen*.'

'Bollocks, he's been trained by Willie Mullins and he's got Paul Townend in the saddle. He'll make the trip.' Kenny said, confidently.

'As long as he hasn't got Pete Townshend on board, then we'll be alright.'

'Who?' Kenny asked.

'Exactly, me arl *meff*,' I replied and we both laughed.

So I stuck my last few coppers on *Burning Victory* and sat back to watch him lose. Like most of Kenny's tips, he tucked himself in with the back-markers as they set off, but I wasn't that worried. It was a couple of miles and, as my arl Fella used to say, the hill usually sorts the wheat from the chaff at Cheltenham. He never actually had a bet, being a man of the Church and all, but that big daft Irish fella did love the *auld* gee-gees.

Anyway, by the time they'd climbed the slope, *Burning Victory* had fallen back to dead last. 'Bloody hell Ken, I thought you could see things from beyond the grave,' I muttered. 'I might as well have put my money on a three-legged donkey.'

'Wait for it,' he said, reminding me of the *auld* days, when Ma used to make us do our homework. I'd be struggling for hours, whilst he'd be grinning from across the room, already finished, balancing two legs of his chair in the air with his arms folded behind his neck.

'I hope you bloody fall, you no good piece of shit,' I said.

'Somebody's *gonna* fall, but it isn't going to be me,' he replied.

'Alright, calm down,' I mumbled, wondering if he was starting.

About four from home and *Burning Victory* finally made his move, but the favourite *Goshen* was still streets ahead. As they reached the second from last, it had to be ten lengths between them. 'For fucks sake, Kenny. I was going to have that one as well.'

'Wait for it,' he said, for the second time. And sure enough, *Goshen* didn't even lift his feet as he hit the final fence. He stumbled through it like a *bladdered Farder Bunloaf*, unseating his rider and throwing him into the air.

61

Burning Victory still had a lot to do. It certainly didn't help when the riderless horse took up the rails and kept on running like a headless chicken. But somehow, he did enough to beat *Aspire Tower* to the post and win by a couple of lengths.

'What did I tell you my arl *meff*,' Kenny said. 'You can thank me later down the *Willow*.'

Like I said, Kenny wasn't always on form, but when he was *shaping* he was *shaping*. And today was starting to look like one of those days. 'So, who are we having in the next, my arl *meff*?'

'Well, I'd love to give you another long-priced winner, but even if you back *Build-Me-Up-Buttercup* each-way, you'd still be better off with the favourite to win.'

'So should I stick the whole lot on *Saint Roi*?' I asked, more than a little confused. 'On the nose?'

'You said it, not me, my arl *meff*.' Kenny crowed. I hated it when he did this. But that was the problem with talking to your late brother, you couldn't kill the bastard because he was already dead. To make matters worse, it was a lower class race this next one, which usually meant the form book went out the window. In the end, I went with my gut and stuck everything I had on the favourite.

It was a big field and they were like bumper cars as they came up the hill. With three to go, I started to wish I had gone each-way on an outsider. Even though mine, *Saint Roi*, was amongst them, it was absolutely anybody's race. Even when he jumped the last, he wasn't quite in front. But the moment Geraghty put him clear, he always looked like staying on. 'Bloody hell Ken, pinch me now I'm dreaming.'

'There's plenty more where that came from my arl *meff*, but it's getting *auld* in here. I'll tell you another three winners, but for fucks sake, let's go down the Willow for a couple more.'

'Reel them off then, Ken,' I said.

'Swerve the next race, it's too tight to call. Save your money and put it on *Al Boum Photo* in the fourth. I fancy *It Came to Pass* in the fifth and let me see,' he said. 'Ar yes, *Eclair de Beaufeu* in the ten to five.'

'Swerve that,' I protested. 'I fancy *Chosen Mate* in that one.'

'It's your funeral, my arl *meff*.' Kenny laffed. 'But do what you want.'

To be fair, I was hardly listening by then. I'd already filled out the betting slip and the *Judy* behind the counter was proper grinning at me. If I'd been ten years younger, I'd swear she was hoping for a *knee-trembler up the jigger*. 'How much of your winnings do you want to put on, luv?'

'All of it,' I said. 'And can you tell me how much I'll win if they all come in?'

'Let me see,' she said, tapping away at her screen. 'If they all win, you're looking at twenty-one-thousand, eight-hundred and ninety-six pounds. Plus your stake.'

'Enough to solve all my worries and get me *bladdered*.' I laughed.

'I should bloody well hope so,' she replied, giving me those *up the entry eyes* of hers.

'Don't worry, I'll give the *doorman a dropsie* when I come back.' I was so smitten, I didn't even notice them *blert*s had returned, the ones who'd been loitering around the door.

'Calm down or I'll put a fluke's gob on you,' Kenny said, as I backed into them.

But in fairness, they didn't even start. That's when I knew this was going to be a good day. 'Come on my arl *meff*,' I said, turning towards Kenny. 'Last one down the *Willow* is getting them in.'

After a quick stagger across town and an even quicker piss down Hackins Hey, we arrived at the Willow, for the second time that day. Only now it was getting pretty busy, so I had to keep an eye out for the *Deli Mob*. I was giving everyone these proper *snarky* glances as I went to the bar, but seeing as ar Kenny had been picking the winners, it was the least I could do to get the drinks in.

We got down to watching the fourth and, call me superstitious, but this one was called the Magners Chase. So that's what I ordered, a Magners and whiskey chaser. I wish I'd thought of it earlier. There was definitely something in it because my horse, *Al Boum Photo*, ended up winning by such a short head, they needed a photo finish to separate them. Now I *was* getting proper excited. A little too excited for my arl nerves, so I went outside for a couple of *loosies*. I couldn't believe they didn't let you have one inside these days.

'Two more and you're all paid up,' Ken said.

'Shut up and *gisalite* will you?' I replied, after all, I didn't want him jinxing it.

By the time I got back inside, they were already off in the next one. I was proper *under the arm* by then and my nose was dripping like a *glass blowers arse*. Having had the *Bombay Crud* of late, it wasn't only going to be my nose dripping, if I didn't scarper off to the *clossit*. When I arrived, just in the nick of time I might add, I saw a couple of *meff*s finishing up a score by the urinals. Now, I wasn't sure which one of those *trainspotters* fancied himself as the train and which one was the tunnel, but the skinny one in the baseball cap smashed straight into me on my way to the stall.

'Fucking watch where you're going, *auld* man,' he said.

'Picking up his precious baggy and putting it back under his hat.'

Believe it or not, I could've put this *blert*'s eye in a sling in a doddle. But not at that moment in time because I desperately needed a Brad Pitt. So, I let it slide for both ar sakes and got on with my business. I won't bore you with the details, but it wasn't the job which was a total pain in the arse, it was the paperwork afterwards. By the time I emerged, the *clossit* was completely empty and the race was well and truly over. Staggering my way back into the bar, I was desperately hoping ar Kenny would tell me the result.

'Well?' I said, as I planted myself down by the telly.

'Came in at sixty-six to one,' he muttered.

'You're having a bloody laugh aren't you?' I said, unable to believe what I was hearing

'Nope, look up there on the screen for yourself my ar meff.'

And true enough, he was right. Which meant just one to go. 'So, Chosen Mate in the last and we're all done.' I *laffed*.

'Don't get your hopes up,' Kenny said. 'I've already seen Eclair de Beaufeu win this one and you know how I see things from beyond the grave.'

I sat there, my head buried in my hands, wondering why I hadn't listened to him. After all, he'd been right every time so far. I could barely look as the race got underway. Round the bend, up the hill and into the final stages they went. My heart quickened with each fall of their hooves. Just as Kenny predicted, Eclair de Beaufeu was absolutely bossing it. She wasn't out in front, but she was holding centre ground and you could see Sean O'Keefe was holding her back.

With two left to jump she rose well, but something happened on her landing. *Jan Maat*, whose jockey just happened to be in the same colours, cut across and took the wind out of her sails. 'Ha, you didn't see that coming, did you Kenny,' I jeered.

The chasing pack closed the gap and *Chosen Mate* emerged in front with only one to go. 'Don't you fucking fall now, you bastard,' I screamed.

She leapt the last like a salmon swimming upstream. By now I'd got the Racing Post rolled up in my hand and I was smacking my own arse with it. Two furlongs out and she was still a couple of lengths clear. 'Come on my beauty.'

Now, I know what you're thinking. She pulled up lame and ar Kenny's horse came back from the dead and pipped her at the post. Well, you'd be fucking wrong, just like my arl *meff* was. She stayed on well and if anything she was

67

pulling away at the finishing post. Having started the day with just a couple of *Firminos* to my name, I'd only gone and won twenty *Stevie G's*.

Needless to say, I was in fucking *La-La Land*.

Chapter 7
Richie Kennedy
13th March 2020

I was surprised how professional it all seemed when I arrived. Not because it was women's football. I'd managed a couple of *gerls* over the years, but they were all in the Super League. I didn't have time to do my homework on Merseyrail Ladies but, by the look of the place, I would've said they were just one league below. Ar Kenny would've definitely approved, anyway. The Admiral Park Recreational ground was the site of the original *Royal* in Toxteth. It was knocked down just after ar Kenny was born, but it was a place of legend. It was where my arl Fella watched the sixty-six World Cup Final. It was one of his favourite stories. Apparently, he wasn't quite old enough to get served, but the landlord turned a blind-eye, seeing as it was a special occasion and all. He got so *bladdered*, he was spewing up chunks when Ken Wolstenholme uttered those immortal words. Still, even though he was a Belfast boy at heart, it was the best day of his life he used to say, other than the day he met my Ma and the days we were born.

By the time I found a good *spec*, I suddenly remembered walking past here some thirty years ago, before I left Merseyside. Back then you were more likely to find *a ruck on the parapet* than a game of footy. Somebody had clearly spent some money clearing this place up. It had modern changing facilities, small undercover technical areas for the coaches and, most importantly, a safe place to park my beloved car.

Both teams were already on the pitch by the time I arrived at the touch-line. Amber's team were wearing blue as they did a little *ticky-tacky* warm up. Ar Kenny would not have liked that. The blue shirts, I mean, not the warm-up drill. Amber had a great first touch, but I couldn't get over her size. I noticed her muscular physique when we first met down the docks, but next to the other girls she looked massive. As the drill changed to a bit of *keep-ball*, it suddenly became clear she knew exactly how to use her weight advantage too. If she wasn't my niece, I'd have probably called her a bully.

A few minutes later and the game kicked off. Both teams started dead cagey, with Amber's team pretty much parking the team bus in front of the goal. Although they'd lined up with just the three central defenders, the full-backs were soon pushed so far back, it started to look like five, four, one. With Amber completely isolated up front.

To be fair, I could see why they did it. Every time the ball went forward she would tirelessly chase it down. Harrying

70

defenders, shoulder charging them out the way. She was a proper menace. But still, she lacked support. As the game developed, she became less and less involved. The away team settled into a possession based game, pressing the home team higher and higher up the field and strangling any outlet passes which they tried to send forward. They soon opened the scoring with a free header from a corner and, by half-time, Merseyrail went two down. To be honest, they only had themselves to blame.

I gave Amber a wave as she left the field. Whilst she acknowledged me with a little nod, she was clearly not in the mood for smiling. I thought about going over and having a word with the coach. If they would just push the full-backs up a bit higher, they would suddenly discover they had enough width to escape the press. Then, if the number ten would only get a bit closer to Amber, she'd definitely get a bit of loose change from Amber's hold-up play and the goals would surely follow. Every ball which went anywhere near Amber she won easily. I wasn't saying it because she was ar Kenny's daughter, it was just so frustrating to see such talent going to waste like that. I even took a few steps towards the technical area, before I thought better of it. I realised my opinion probably wouldn't be welcomed.

The second-half came and, unfortunately, it was much of the same. Pretty soon two became three with a miserable own goal. Merseyrail were lucky not to go four down when the away team missed a penalty. Then a hospital pass of a clearance came sailing over the halfway line and bounced between the opposing team's lines. Amber muscled her way in, shrugging off the holding midfielder like a rag doll, but still she had nowhere to go. The ball was bouncing awkwardly and one of their centre backs had come out to clean it up. A clever flick with her right foot and Amber ended up lobbing her, but now the ball seemed too far ahead. She had no right to get there first, but her raw pace saw her narrowly beat the last defender, pushing it past her with a toe-poke off her left boot. She almost lost her footing as she went past her, probably on the wrong side to be honest. In order to keep her balance, she was forced to go the long way round. It made the advancing keeper odds-on favourite to make the save. I'm no centre-forward, but with the ball still fizzing around, I would've probably blasted it from there. However, Amber regained her composure and patiently waited for the keeper to commit herself, before deftly looping a half-volley which sailed over the goalie's head and bounced twice before it trickled into the net. The hairs on the back of my neck stood up. It was an absolute *worldy*.

It was the sort of goal which could turn a game. The away team's heads dropped, Merseyrail finally pushed the full-backs forward and used the full-width of the park. A few minutes later, they were awarded a corner. When the ball came high across the six-yard box, there was only ever going to be one winner. Amber didn't just get above the central defender, she got her head over the ball and drilled it down with such force, it still went into the roof of the net after bouncing off the turf. Three-two! Suddenly, it was game on.

There was one last almighty push. Amber broke free and drilled one against the post, but the linesman's flag was already up for off-side. The last few minutes were so frantic, it was more like pinball than football. But unfortunately, Merseyrail had left it too late. The ref blew for full-time about two minutes too early for the home team to grab what would've been a well-deserved equaliser. As the teams went in, I could see Amber's coach wanted to bring them together, but I couldn't wait any longer, so I ran out onto the park to meet her. I say ran, I probably made a total arse of myself. What is it our Kenny used to say, "You couldn't catch a pig in a jigger, Richie."

'Hey, Amber. It's me, Richie,' I said, awkwardly, hoping she hadn't forgotten my name already.

'I know, it was only yesterday.' She smiled.

'Sorry, I just wanted to say well done,' I panted, breathlessly. 'You were amazing!'

'Well done?' she said, untucking her shirt and rolling down her socks. 'We bloody well lost.'

'But through no fault of yours,' I added. 'That first goal was something else, they both were.'

'Look *gissus* five to get changed and you can take us out if you want. I think the coach wants a word first.'

'I wouldn't bother if I was you,' I said. 'With the coach I mean. If he'd only pushed the full-backs up earlier and told your number ten to get close to you, then you'd probably have won eight-nil.'

'Exactly,' she said. 'But he'll fine me if I don't go in straight away.'

Chapter 8
Wayne Kennedy
13th March 2020

For an awful moment I thought there was going to be a steward's enquiry, after all, ar Kenny's horse had pretty much been run out of the race by *Jan Maat*. It seemed to take forever for the result to be confirmed, but the moment it flashed up as *weighed in* on the big screen, it was like somebody had just got the drinks in.

There I was, dancing in the middle of the ale house. Anyone would've thought I was in *der bloody Ippy*. I was bashing into *meff*s left, right and centre, doing a full Irish jig. Drinks were sloshing, people were staring, but they could all piss off to the *One-eyed City* if they wanted to start because I'd just won twenty bags of sand.

'What did I tell you, me arl *meff*?' Kenny said.

'To put it on that bloody French filly in the last, if my memory serves me right?' I replied.

'Charming,' he said. 'I give you four winners and all you want to talk about is the one I got wrong. You've bloody won, now get the drinks in and we can go see the arl *Fella* like a couple of millionaires.'

I reached into my pocket to give the betting slip a little kiss and that's when I realised. 'Fucking hell, Ken. What have you done with it?' I said. 'That's not bloody funny.'

But ar Kenny didn't say a word.

All of a sudden, I'd gone from being completely *brewstered*, dancing in the pub, to a *parlytic meff* without enough *lolly* to pay the *latch-lifter*. And by now, people were proper staring. 'Where was you when I had der coppers?' I slurred, stumbling toward the back room.

That's when I saw him. The little *blert* who'd stolen my betting slip. It had to be him. The little crack-head, doing his dirty deals in the *clossit*. When he bumped into us earlier, it obviously hadn't been an accident. He'd been dipping my pockets. It was the oldest trick in the book. Now, I really wished ar Kenny was there to back us up, even though he was more mouth than trousers, I could've still used the moral support. But in all honesty, that had been the problem for the past thirty years. Sure, I heard him in my head most of the time, but I couldn't really rely on him. Not when it mattered. So, I went charging in there, hoping my reputation would precede me and this *blert* would get cold feet. 'Hand it over then, I don't want to involve your fucking relations.'

The little *meff* just stared back at me. 'Hand over what?'

'Hand over what?' I asked. 'The betting slip you dipped out of my pockets earlier.'

But the little *blert* just started *gassing*. 'Go home *auld* man, I didn't steal your bus pass.'

Now, he left me no choice. Nobody mugs me off like that, so I steamed in with a couple of jabs. I realised I wasn't exactly match-fit, but usually *meffs* like him backed-down and folded if you went in early. Well, I don't know if you've ever had the feeling, when you're *proper marmalising* some *blert* and it's just not doing anything, but let me tell you it's pretty humiliating. Before I knew it, I'd slipped on one of them little blue soaps they put in urinals for *Kopites* like me to piss on and I'd fallen on my arse. To make matters worse, this *meff* was stood over me laughing. To be fair, he could've pulled down his zipper and proper took a piss on me, but he didn't. He just turned out his pockets and said, 'I didn't steal your fucking betting slip you stupid *auld blert.*'

And there I was, lying in the *clossit*, stinking of piss without a penny in my pocket. Ar kid had deserted us, my arl Fella was still in a coma, I still owed the Deli Mob twenty bags and I hadn't got a hope in hell of sorting it out.

That's when I heard ar Kenny finally pipe up. 'Right idea, but wrong *blerts* my arl *meff.*' And of course he was right. It wasn't that *trainspotter* who'd *chief*ed my betting slip after

77

all. It was those two *blert*s in the betting shop who'd overheard me talking about my winnings. So that's where I headed, staggering out of the *Willow* and straight over to the bookies, hoping I might catch them before they cashed it in.

'Oh my god, look at you,' the pretty lass behind the counter said. 'I think you might have overdone the celebrating.'

'Celebrating?' I replied. 'That's not what I'd call it.'

'Well, you'll have to clean yourself up tomorrow if you want to take me out.'

'Tomorrow?' I asked, completely confused.

'Like I told your brothers earlier,' she continued. 'If you want it paid out in cash you'll have to wait until tomorrow.'

'What are you talking about?' I asked.

'Well, I thought it was funny when your brothers came in on your behalf. But seeing as they were insisting on cash and, we don't keep that much on site, my boss said he'd have to do a bank run in the morning.'

'Two of them, you said?'

'Yep.' The *Judy* nodded.

'But I've only got one brother.' I replied. 'And he wouldn't be seen dead in a betting shop.'

'That's not entirely true, is it?' Kenny said, chewing away at my ear.

'*Shurrup!*' I snapped, without even realising I was speaking out loud.

'Sorry, I wasn't starting, luv,' the *gerl* said. 'So were these two just your mates then?'

That's when I realised something terrible, something even worse than losing twenty grand. 'I haven't really got any mates, darling.'

'Oh,' she said, looking dead sorry for me. 'Well, this has only ever happened once before, but last time we got the police involved and they did a handwriting check. I'm not sure if we paid out at all in the end, but I know the fraudsters didn't get away with it.'

'Oh, that makes me feel so much better,' I replied.

'Do you want me to call them and we can contest the claim when these two come back tomorrow? I'd be happy to vouch for you.'

'Nah, I've never had much time for the *bizzies*, luv.' I said. 'Leave it to me, I'll sort it out.'

Chapter 9
Richie Kennedy
13th March 2020

Despite my intentions being entirely honourable, I couldn't help but feel like a bit of a pervert, waiting outside the ladies' changing rooms. When Amber eventually emerged, I hardly recognised her. She'd tied her hair back with a flowery *scrunchie* and she was wearing a tight little strappy top with some dusty pink shorts, which I had thought was a skirt for a moment. I wondered if *skorts* was the right term, but to be honest, I could barely think straight with the way they made her legs look so long and muscular.

'Hiya,' I said, desperately trying to regain my composure. 'So what did the coach say?'

'He's going to drop me next week,' Amber replied, despondently.

'You're kidding aren't you?' I asked.

'Yeah. But only back into the hole. So the *gerl* who was playing at number ten can push up ahead of us. That's how we usually line-up. He just wanted to give me a chance upfront today. I've been begging him all season.'

'It might help the team that way around, but it's a total waste of your talent playing you further down the field,' I remarked. 'Your second goal reminded me of Emile Heskey, but even he couldn't have scored that first one.'

'Are you kidding?' Amber said, shaking her head. 'Heskey was my favourite player growing up.'

'So many people overlooked him,' I said. 'He was totally underrated if you ask me. He did so much hard work, which freed up his teammates to score the goals. Just ask Michael Owen.'

'Trust me, I would if I had his number.' Amber smiled.

'Isn't he a bit old for you?' I asked.

'Oh no, I like the older man,' she replied.

'You know I was part of the Heskey transfer,' I said, opening the car door, realising we were heading dangerously close to flirting territory again.

'What?' She laughed, as I went around to the other side. 'As part-exchange?'

'No, I was his agent,' I replied.

'I knew you weren't a player when you ran across the pitch,' Amber said. 'Couldn't catch a pig in a jigger, you!'

'Hey, that's a bit unkind.' I said. Although by now she definitely reminded me of ar Ken.

'So that's why you pretended to know my Ma and everything?' Amber asked.

'Pretended?' I said, worried she might have worked it out already.

'You've come to scout me haven't you?' she asked, grinning from ear to ear. 'Obviously I'd prefer Liverpool, but as you've probably guessed, I'll wear a blue shirt if I have to.'

'Sorry Amber, but there's something else,' I said, nervously.

'So, is this just a date then?'

'If that's what you want to call it,' I said, trying to buy myself a little more time. I wasn't even sure if she was ar Kenny's daughter and I certainly wasn't ready to break the news to Ma. 'So where should I take you?'

'To be honest, I'm happy with a Maccy's,' she said, sounding more like a *Tocky* than I ever could. 'I get proper starving after a match.'

I swear down, if I hadn't suspected her of being my niece and my divorce was already settled, I would've probably asked her to marry me right there and then. It's not that I even liked McDonald's or anything. It's just Amber was different to other *gerls*. Like the uncompromising way she played the game, she was straightforward.

'Are you sure?' I said.

'What's wrong with a Maccy's?' Amber asked.

'Nothing at all,' I replied, pulling out of the car park and punching the nearest McDonald's into my sat-nav. I don't know if I was showing off, or just finding it hard to concentrate with her legs on show, but I ended up sticking it into self-driving mode. Thankfully my Tesla had automatic braking, or I probably would've ended up killing a couple of stray cats on our way down Park Road. 'So what are you having?' I said, as we arrived safely beneath the golden arches.

'Three cheeseburgers, two Big Macs, a portion of fries and a McFlurry please, darl,' she replied.

Once again, I couldn't fathom where she was going to put it all, but I obliged all the same and ordered myself a coffee. Amber had already demolished the three cheeseburgers by the time it had cooled enough to take a sip. 'Look, there's something I need to tell you,' I said, nervously fiddling with the little wooden stirrer and the tiny packets of sugar. 'I might not have been entirely truthful when we met.'

'You're not married are you?' she asked.

'Erm, well, kind of,' I squirmed, not quite ready to answer questions about my divorce. 'Technically I am, but not for much longer.'

'It's a bit like the offside rule. You either are or you're not,' she said, well on the way to polishing off her Big Mac now too. 'I'm finishing my fries, but you can consider this date over.'

'If you must know, my soon to be ex-wife signed the divorce papers yesterday,' I said. 'That's not what I was lying about.'

'Ok, I'm proper confused now,' she said. 'But I'm not going to waste this McFlurry either. So you've got another thirty seconds to start making sense.'

'You know when I said ar Kenny was one of your Ma's boyfriends at school,' I stuttered.

She looked up from her ice-cream and finally I had her undivided attention. 'Yeah.'

'Well, he actually was her *only* boyfriend at school,' I said, deliberately stressing the word *only*.

'Oh,' Amber said, with ice-cream now dribbling down her chin.

'Her only boyfriend, just shy of thirty-one years ago,' I said, repeating myself one more time.

'So?' Amber said. 'Things were different then.'

'But how old are you?' I asked.

'Thirty.' she said, scraping her spoon around the bottom of her ice-cream. 'Oh, now I get it.'

'Do you?' I said, worried she was still a yard behind the pace.

'I've heard of guys expecting a bit of *how's your father* on the first date, but I've never had one who wanted to play who's your uncle.'

'Exactly!' I said, realising the penny had finally dropped.

Chapter 10
Wayne Kennedy
13th March 2020

As I stumbled out of the bookies, my legs could hardly hold me. Still, for some strange reason, I staggered on. Past the *arl Madge, der Ippy* and *der Black House*. I saw them, I mean I really saw them. Even though I'd seen them almost every day of my life, I hadn't really noticed how amazing they were until now. They say you never notice what's right on the end of your nose. Well, forty-eight years I'd lived in *der Pool,* and only now did I realise, I was blessed to live in the most beautiful city in the world. It's a funny *auld* thing life, but when the sky is caving in and you're absolutely broken, you suddenly become all poetic.

Gerrup dere La! De knocker-ups sleeps light;
Dawn taps yer winder, ends anudder night;
And Lo! de dog-eared moggies from next-door
Tear up de jigger fer an early fight.

Half-dreaming, half-par'latic on me back;
O Jeez, another day before yiz Jack;
And groping for de ciggies by me bed
I sought de drag dat frees me from de rack.

I carried on to *where the bugs wore clogs* and copped a
squat on an *auld* bench beside the water. I tried to roll the
perfect *loosie*, but no matter how hard I tried, I couldn't get it
right. Some were too tight and others too loose. To be honest,
I think I'd been trying to string my *burn* out for so long, it
had just gone dry. Watching the ferries coming in across the
Mersey, I smoked them all and wound up with a sore throat.
Otis Redding could've sang *Sitting on the Dock of the Bay*
and my worries still wouldn't have rolled away with the tide.
I felt dog-tired. Not just with losing my betting slip earlier,
but with life itself.

De Werld's just like dat pub in 'Ackins 'Ey,
De towels on de taps all bleedin' day;
Yer time is up before a decent sup
Dat mingy Landlord, Fate, says: "On yer way."

Many's the Fella dat I use' ter mug;
Ard cases who could bevvy by the jug.
Dey've cadged dere last latch-lifter out a me
And werms live jockey-bar inside dere lug.

Before I knew it, I was wandering the streets again, reciting the bloody Rubaiyat. I'd have done anything to hear ar Kenny's voice, but he'd completely deserted us. It happened like that from time to time. One minute he was there to hold my hand, getting me into trouble, the next he was gone. When all along, it was me who was supposed to be holding his hand, especially on that fateful day, all those years ago.

So shun de Cokes and join me in de Pub;
But 'urry, Life is short, aye dere's the rub.
De Liver Bird's already on de wing
And Time's de one thing, mates, yer' ll never sub.

O Thou who didst wid Therlfalls and wid Gin,
Allow us all to take life on de chin;
Are you de self-same unrelenting Sod
Who slips us all de final Mickey-Finn?

I must've wandered around the whole city. I think part of me wanted to bump into the *Deli Mob*, just to get it over and done with. Ok, so the fat lady hadn't quite started to sing just yet. I could always wait outside the bookies in the morning and catch them *meff*s red-handed, but if I'd learnt anything down the *Willow* earlier, it was my fighting days were over.

So come, me mates, and fill yer boots wid Beer;
You may be in Ford Cemetry next year;
Termorrer? Listen, La, it never comes,
Let Fally drown yer sorrows, it's de gear,

Poor Uncle Tom no longer bears de 'od,
Unless ee's still a brickie up wid God;
And Clayballs, Guardian of de Mystery
In Smithie lies, six feet below de sod!

There was a time when I could've taken on the whole Park End, but those days had gone. I couldn't beat one of them *blert*s in the *clossit*, let alone two. And I wasn't going to wait for the *bizzies* to sort out my problems. It's not like the *Deli Mob* were going to put it on the slate until that load of time wasters came good.

Dey say dat pile a bricks in Calderstones
Was once a Druid's doss-house full of thrones;
But dig around where kids now sport and play
And all you'll find's discarded rags and bones.

90

Alas dat Rose should vanish with me mate
And leave them unpaid bevvies on de slate;
With all dem fag-ends, soaked beyond repair
And all dem hours lost through minutes late.

Skirting through Dingle and past *der Cazzy*, I turned towards home. I hoped I might get a word from ar Kenny, as I crossed St Agnes field. After all, it was the scene of most of *ar* crimes as kids. They were the days. Smoking *loosies* and *sagging off skewl*. Until ar arl Fella found out and gave us what for. He made us work on his allotment for an entire week. Still, it could've been worse. He could've told ar Ma and we'd have ended up doing it for two weeks with a sore arse.

And as as a lad I seldom went ter school;
Just bare-arsed round de streets of Liverpool.
Lost all me coloured oldies down de grid
And skipped de leckies to stick of Doom!

O Christ I'd pawn me heart in Rotherhams
And even swap de buses for de trams
For a vintage butty spread wid Hartley's Jam
Or a day at Blackler's Grotto wid me Mam.

There wasn't as much as a whisper from *ar* kid, so I continued into *Tockie*. I went through those big black gates one final time, down the gravel path and round the bend. I sat there beside his memorial and tried to summon the courage to say the things I needed to say. Who knows, maybe I wanted to offer an exchange. My life for his.

O for a cob of chuck beneat de boughs
The Football Echoe and a pan of scouse;
A Black and Tan, and Maggie sweatin' bricks
In Sevvy's rough, dat's Paradise enough.

With the gates about to be locked for the night, I gave up the ghost and made my way back home. I stumbled through the door and slumped down on the sofa, switching on the telly. The last thing I wanted to watch was the bloody news, but I didn't have a choice. It was playing on every channel. Apparently this virus had got much worse since yesterday. To be honest, I wasn't really bothered what that *whacker* Johnson had to say, but one of those headlines which flashed on the bottom of the screen caught my attention. They'd only gone and postponed the football season. Bloody typical. Thirty years since Liverpool won the league, finally we were

twenty-five points clear, and they'd decided to call the whole
thing off.

De Ref no question makes of rights or wrongs
Just makes de rules up as e goes along.
And many a foul as penalised de weak
While many an off-side rule supports de strong.

It might've sounded trivial, but I think that was the final
straw. I went to the kitchen and took down the bottle of
Captain Morgan's I'd been saving for the fifteenth of April.
The anniversary of Kenny's death. Then I rummaged around
the cupboards for some pain-killers. Pens, paper, *plazzy* bags,
it seemed I owned all sorts of useless crap, but I was
buggered if I could find any *Gary Abletts*. I could've sworn
ar Lozzle brought some over with my shopping yesterday.
Who knows, maybe ar Kenny had *chiefed* them.

Life's like a game of pitch'n'toss
But youre de meg dat's thrown up be de Boss
It's heads a penny', but de 'ead is yours;
Somehow you find dat every call's a loss.

When I was young half of me time was spent
Up jowlers playing 'ookey wid de rent;
Was always skint and found I use'ter go
Down de same jiggers as whereup I went.

Dats put der top ut.

Feeling proper down the banks, I gave up and got stuck into that bottle of rum. I thought it might take a while, but I demolished it in under an hour, flitting between sorrow and rage as I continued to hunt for the painkillers. Fed up with all the crashing and banging, I took a pen and paper and just started writing. Who knows, maybe it was *Captain Morgan* himself flowing through my veins, but thirty years of hurt suddenly started pouring out.

13/03/2020

Dear Ma,

If you're reading this then I'm sorry, but I've let you down again. I know a mother should never have to lose a son, so to lose two must be unimaginable. Believe me when I say there isn't a day goes by when I don't think about ar kid and I don't mean just remember him. I hear him all the time. He's

94

down the pub, in the betting shop and on my shoulder every minute of every day. Especially on match day, where I like to think of him standing in the Kop, cheering on the boys from beyond the grave. Don't get me wrong, Ma, I'm not trying to say he's been holding me back. The truth is, he's been holding me up. He has been for the past thirty years now, but he just couldn't hold onto us any longer. There's not a day goes by when I wish it hadn't been different. I wish it had been me that didn't come home to you on that fateful day, not him. He was an angel and the best centre-forward I've ever seen. He would've made the big time if things had been different, but I know you find that hard to bear. Just like I do.

As for ar arl Fella, I'm sorry I haven't been to see him of late, but I just couldn't face him. It's the look in his eyes. He just looks broken. So please, don't tell him about my passing, not unless you really have to, I couldn't bear it if I finished him off. Could you also tell him it wasn't his fault on that day at the footy. There's nothing he could've, or should've, done differently. He'd taken his boys to the big match, it's what every father should do. He showed us how to become men, how to follow in his footsteps, how to be a family. It's not his fault we never came back whole that day. It was mine. Kenny was ar kid, it's me that should've been watching over him.

95

As for Richie, you were right about him. You always were. He isn't a total whacker, he's a good lad. What he's achieved for himself makes me incredibly proud. After all, he's ar kid and none of us had it easy growing up, least of all him.

Could you also keep an eye on ar Lozzle for us. I know you always do, but I'm sure you know by now how she's been dating a blue-nose. Tell her it doesn't matter. I did tell her myself, but I'm not sure she believed us. And tell her she looks smashing in that coat I bought her. Oh, and by the way, that picture she drew on her fifth birthday wasn't meant to upset you, that's just how she remembers ar Kenny, as a clown. I'm glad she can see him that way, I just wish I could too.

All my love,

ya total waste of space,

Wayne x

After I finished the letter, I made one last concerted effort to find the painkillers, lifting up the sofa to take a look underneath. That's when I realised, I was right about ar Kenny *chiefing* them. I'd been sat on them the whole time. It was exactly the sort of stunt he liked to pull. Hiding stuff right under my nose and *laffing* as I struggled to find it. Besides, I could finally hear him again now too, whispering away in my ear. 'You need to call your brother.'

'Fuck, off!' I shouted, reaching for the tablets with one hand and holding up the sofa with the other. Pissed as a fart, I must've stumbled back and dropped the sofa on my foot. Before I knew it, I'd accidentally tripped over the phone cable and knocked the *tingey* which held it in place onto my head.

So there I was, lying there on the floor with the receiver in my hand and the dialling tone blearing away in my ear. Now, I don't know if I punched in the bloody number or whether it was ar Kenny, but before I realised what had happened, I was calling my loaded little brother to bail me out.

'Wayne, is that you?' he said, when he finally picked up.

'Of course it's bloody me,' I replied. 'Who did you think it was, your other brother?'

'No, Wayne,' Richie replied. 'I just didn't have your landline stored into my phone. I wish you'd just use your mobile like everybody else.'

'Well, it's been cut off ages ago,' I snapped. 'I haven't got money to burn like you.'

'Alright, Wayne,' Richie said. 'If you've just called to sound off whilst you're pissed then you needn't have bothered.'

'It's not that,' I begged. 'I just need some help.'

'With the drinking?' Richie said. 'It's a bit late for that, don't you think?'

'Nah, with the money,' I replied.

'How much do you need this time?' Richie asked.

'A load,' I said. 'A fucking shit-load.'

'How much is a shit-load, Wayne?'

'Twenty bags,' I said. 'But I don't want you to pay my debts.'

'Well that's a relief,' Richie replied. 'After this divorce, I'm not sure I've got twenty grand sat about.'

'You're getting a divorce?' I asked.

'Look, it doesn't matter,' Richie muttered. 'Whatever you need, I'll get it. Just give me time.'

'I don't have time,' I said. 'That's the problem.'

'So what do you suggest then?' Richie asked.

'What I really need is your help with a couple of *meffs*, who turned me over today,' I said. 'Do you think you can manage that?'

'Like I said.' Richie sighed. 'You're my brother. So I've got your back.'

Chapter 11
Wayne Kennedy
14th March 2020

I thought there was something up when ar Kenny told us to back that last horse, only for it to fail at the final hurdle. After all, he'd been *shaping* all day. I started to wonder if this was his plan from the beginning. For me to get so close to settling my debts, I'd end up phoning ar Richie to bail me out. So when I didn't go along with my *arl meff's* set-up, it must've properly pissed in his custard.

Having said all that, somehow, here we were. The two of us, sat in ar Richie's fancy car, hatching a plan. It was like the *auld* days, only better. We were no longer skipping skewl, scarpering across St Agnes field. This was far more dangerous. Still, despite the fact his little *shenanigans* had fallen at the final fence, I couldn't help but think ar Kenny had a hand in things somewhere along the line. Maybe he was even keeping *douse* from above.

After picking us up in *Tockie,* Richie did a little dally down the docks to get his car charged. Now, I don't know if it's possible to get seasick driving past the sea, but I started to feel proper rough. Sweat was hopping out my *arm-holes* and I was shivering like a shagging dog. I began to wonder if I was coming down with that dreaded virus, although it was far more likely to be a hangover from the bottle of *jungle-juice* I'd polished off the night before. 'For fuck's sake. Pull over, will you?' I stuttered.

'You're not going to throw up are you?' Richie snapped. 'Don't you dare do it in the car.'

'I'm not going to be sick, you big *blert*,' I whined, as he came to an abrupt halt. 'I'm just popping to the *offy*. Do want *owt*?'

'It's ten o'clock in the morning,' he replied. 'Take a day off, will you?'

'You take a day off,' I said, nipping into the shop and coming out with a *plazzy* bag full of supplies. I pulled out a cheap bottle of cider and a box of ciggies with a picture of a rotten lung on the front. 'Can you believe they don't do *White Lightening* anymore? And look what they've done to the packets of *Players*.'

'What's this for?' Richie asked. 'Pre-match nerves?'

'Nah, *auld* times,' I said. 'Come on, you're at your Nan's, tuck in.'

Richie didn't hesitate, snatching the cider and taking a healthy swig. 'I wish you would just let me pay them off.'

'Come on, I've got my pride,' I replied, *chiefing* the bottle back before he chugged the lot. 'We don't want you getting over the limit.'

'Drink driving is the least of my worries,' Richie replied, poncing a *loosie*. 'What do you think we'll get for *chiefing* twenty grand?'

'Firstly, it's not *chiefing* if it's ars in the first place,' I replied. 'And secondly, we're not *chiefing* twenty grand, we're *chiefing* a betting slip, worth twenty grand.'

'Fair point. But I could still do without getting a record on this little trip down memory lane of yours,' he said, refusing anymore of the cider when I offered him back the bottle.

'Come on, what else are brothers for?' I replied. 'If not sticking up for each other in a fight?'

'Fair enough,' Richie slurred and I started to wonder if he was already bladdered. 'So where's this betting shop anyway?'

'Just next to the *Twelfth Man,*' I said. 'Do you know it?'

'Nah, but my car does,' Richie replied, punching it into his sat-nav.

'Fucking whacker!' I shouted and we both *laffed*.

In the end, I got him to park across the street from the *alehouse*. We could still see the entrance to the betting shop, but I didn't want us right outside in case we got caught on camera if things got *airyated*. I looked up at the sign of the *Twelfth Man* and smiled. I couldn't help but think it was a good sign, a sign *ar* Kenny was watching us. Not that there was a lot to see, it was a bit boring at first, like being on a stakeout. Me and ar kid could've been *Starsky and Hutch,* only we didn't have any meatball subs or whatever boloney they used to eat in those *auld* American cop movies. Instead, we just sat there, lighting up *loosies*, one after the other. Trying to calm the *auld* shakes.

'Do you even remember what these *meffs* look like?' Richie asked.

'Not exactly.' I shrugged. 'But don't worry about that.'

'Well, at the risk of stating the bleeding obvious,' Richie scowled. 'How the hell are we going to know who they are?'

'Don't laff,' I said, a little bit embarrassed. 'But ar Kenny's going to give me the nod.'

'Oh, for fuck sake, Wayne!' Richie moaned. 'This is getting ridiculous now.'

'What?' I exclaimed. 'Don't you believe he's still up there, watching over us?'

'It's not that,' Richie said, keen to change the subject. 'You're flicking fag ash on my seats. They're genuine vegan leather.'

'Vegan leather?' I remarked, almost pissing myself. 'I always thought you bought your clothes from Carnaby Street, but now I've heard it all.'

'*Shurrup*,' Richie said.

'Nah, you *shurrup*,' I replied.

'Don't get *airyated*,' Richie continued. 'I'm doing you a favour here.'

But I wasn't. Two *blerts* in blue shirts had just come bowling round the corner and ar Kenny's voice was ringing in my ear. 'Look lively.'

'That's them,' I said, throwing my *loosie* out the window. 'Come on, get your coat you've pulled.'

Now, I'll give Richie his due. We all knew he couldn't catch a pig in a jigger, but he was out there like a shot. He didn't even give it any foreplay. He went straight to number one, swinging punches at the big fella's head like a proper Toxteth terrier. Only just like when we were kids, he couldn't punch a hole in a wet Echo that one. So unless his plan was to wear down this *meff's* fists with his face, things weren't exactly going his way.

I would've stepped in straight away, but I had his mate to deal with. Now, I'd be lying if I said there wasn't the slightest bit of performance pressure hovering over my head, after my disappointing outing in the *alehouse* yesterday. But I needn't have worried. When I hung one on this *meff*, it connected so sweet, he fell to the ground like an out-of-form striker looking for a penalty. I suppose it must have been *brewer's droop* affecting me down the *Willow* and not *auld*

103

age after all. Even Mo Salah forgot to wear his shooting boots sometimes.

When I originally saw the colour of their shirts, I had assumed these *meffs* were blue-noses, but as I stared at my man lying prone on the pavement, I realised he was a different kind of scum. A Chelsea fan. Now, I really should've gone and helped ar kid at this stage, but this was too good to miss. Besides, it wouldn't do the *whacker* any harm if the big *fella* got a couple of licks in before I rescued him.

So there I was, pounding away at this cockney scum-bag, when I suddenly realised he wasn't the one packing heat. And I'm not talking about the betting slip. Richie had finally *purra flukes gob* on his man, who stumbled back with a nosebleed, reached into his pocket and pulled out a blade. 'Fucking Chelsea scum,' I shouted. 'I should've known you lot wouldn't fight fair.'

There was a stomach curdling silence as they eyed each other up. It was like watching a penalty at the Anfield Road end. The blade might only have been a Stanley knife but this *blert* was still odds-on to score. Richie reached into his own pocket and pulled out a phone. 'Fucking hell, Richie, you might as well have brought a knife to a gun fight,' I yelled.

My blood turned cold. *How could I have let this happen?*
I'd already let one of my brothers die. I left my man lying on
the ground and started to peg it, ready to dive between them.
That's when I realised, I'd happily take a blade or a bullet for
ar Richie, even if he was a total whacker. But as it turned out,
I didn't have to.

Even in the heat of the moment, I realised *ar* kid would be
dining out on this story for the rest of his life. I could hear
him telling his mates down some posh wine bar, how he was
about to die at the hands of the entire Chelsea Football Firm
when, like Michael Knight, he summoned his car to the
rescue.

It's not that ar Richie's car actually hit this *meff* hard, you
understand. Not with all the safety features he was constantly
boasting about. It sort of ploughed through the back of his
knees like an aging centre-back lumbering across the field to
take out a fleet-footed winger. But it was enough to make
him stumble back across the bonnet. I didn't wait for the ref
to blow the whistle, wading in with a high tackle of my own,
leaving him flat-out on his back. Then I rifled through his
pockets, took back the betting slip which was rightfully mine
and dragged him to the curb-side with his mate, so they
didn't get themselves run over. There was no way I was
doing a life-stretch for these two *meffs*. That's when I caught

sight of Richie, still staring at his phone as if he'd just got a text message from ar kid Kenny. 'Look at you standing there like one of the Lewises,' I said. 'Get in that car and fucking drive.'

Unlike the movies, there weren't any loud noises as we sped away. A slight squeal of the tyres and a touch of brake dust maybe. That's electric cars for you, weirder than a *clockwerk* orange. After that we must have sat there in total silence for at least a quarter of a mile, until ar Richie started muttering away. 'What if they call the *bizzies,* it's illegal to leave the scene of an accident.'

'It was no fucking accident,' I said, confidently. 'And nobody's calling the fucking *bizzies.*'

We sat in silence for a minute longer. Then we both just burst out laughing. I don't know why ar Richie was creasing up, but for me it was a kind of catharsis. Yesterday had been the worst day of my life. Well, the worst day since ar Kenny died. But in many ways, I think it'd done me good. I'd finally hit rock bottom. It hadn't been the first time I'd thought that way, but this time was different. There was a moment when I was actually ready to throw in the towel and join him.

Well, if I died later today, then I'd be a happy man because kicking the shit out of those two little *blerts* with my whacker of a brother was the best therapy I'd ever had. It wasn't because I was a violent bastard. Or an angry one. Even though both of those things had been true over the years. It was because I'd finally saved ar kid. Okay, so it might not have been ar Kenny, but it might just go some way to making amends. Maybe I could finally stop blaming myself. With enough splosh to clear my debts, it was also a chance at a new beginning. Maybe I could get off the lush and stop working for her *Maj*. Maybe I could get a real job. Help people. Make my *auld* folks proud. Who knows, after thirty years of blaming each other, maybe I could even make things right with ar Richie. Maybe we could become close again. Like brothers should be. Like we used to be. And maybe that's what I wanted to say to ar kid. It's just a shame it didn't come out that way. Those feelings were still too raw, too fragile to voice out loud. So what I actually said was, 'You did well, *La*.' Then I gave him a playful dig on the arm.

Richie winced, he'd obviously taken a bit of a pasting because of me. 'Best you cash that betting slip in somewhere else. Somewhere closer to *Tockie,* so we've got home-field advantage if they try to track us down.'

'Nobody's going to track us down,' I replied, ruling a line under the whole incident. 'Now, let me buy you dinner down the *cokes* to say thanks. After all, I've got twenty bags burning a hole in my pocket.'

'Fine,' Richie replied. 'But we need to call ar Lozzle first. I've got something important to say.'

'This better not be about you buying your clothes in Carnaby Street.' I added, unable to resist.

'Very funny,' Richie said. 'You do know it's the twenty-first century and nobody talks like that anymore?'

'Of course I do,' I said. After all, nobody needed to remind me I'd spent far too long living in the past. 'Come on, let's go see the arl Fella though first.'

Chapter 12
Lauren Kennedy
14th March 2020

The day started dead *brill*. Ar Giles was supposed to be taking us to Goodison Park for the Merseyside derby, apparently his arl Fella had reserved a box and everything. However, despite being really keen to finally meet his *auld* folks, another part of me was dreading it. Family loyalties and all. Even though I didn't really like footy, once a red always a red.

Needless to say, I was over the moon when Giles called to tell me the match was cancelled. Instead, he wanted me to catch a ferry across the Mersey and meet him at Woodside. It was all a bit mysterious, typical Giles, but I had a pretty good idea of what was about to happen next. He'd already told me his *auld* folks had a nice place on the Wirral, so I wasn't surprised when he greeted me at Birkenhead in his flash new company car, wearing an equally flash designer suit. But after doing a little scenic tour of the peninsular, we ended up heading onto the motorway and started cruising down South. Before I knew it, we were rolling up the drive of this huge country estate near Chester, which looked like Downton Abbey, only bigger. It had *auld* iron gates, giant statues, topiary in the shape of peacocks, the whole *bloody* shooting match. There were even some *meffs* playing croquet on the lawn. 'This is never your parents' gaff is it?' I asked.

'This?' Giles said, completely creasing up. 'This is a hotel and spa Lozzle.'

'So why are we here?' I sniggered. 'You'd better not have invited me away for a dirty weekend. I haven't even packed a nightie.'

'You'll see,' Giles said, grinning from ear to ear.

When we stepped inside, it was obvious the silver fox waiting in the lobby was ar Giles arl Fella. The resemblance was startling. 'So here she is, Lauren isn't it?' he said, beaming like a Cheshire cat. 'The one Giles has been telling us all about.'

'Behave, Dad.' Giles said, looking a little embarrassed.

'It is a pleasure to meet you Mr Gilbert.' I stuttered, I couldn't quite remember ar Giles' second name for a second, it was a lot to take in.

'Please call me David,' he replied, kissing me on the cheek.

'You better watch him,' Giles said, 'He fancies himself that one.'

'That's probably where you get it from then,' I said, directing my attention to the lady next to him, hoping for at least a smile of recognition.

'And this is my Mum, Sandra,' Giles said, coming to my rescue after what felt like a long, judgemental silence.

She had to be fifty, but a good fifty if you know what I mean. Her eyebrows looked like they'd been drawn on a little too high and her forehead barely moved, which made me realise it was probably full of Botox. And if I was being really bitchy, I could say the way her boobs heaved out of her dress made it pretty obvious she'd had her tits done too.

Moving on to the restaurant, we made it through a couple of rounds of drinks and our starters before she said a word to us. She just kept shooting us these really dirty looks across the table. I knew there had to be a reason why ar Giles was still single. He had a good job, he was great looking and it was obvious he came from a bit of splosh. In my experience, there was always a catch when it came to men like him and this was obviously it. The arl *gerl* from hell who clearly thought no *Judy* was good enough for her precious son. It wasn't something which needed explaining to me, after all, I had two older brothers to put the frighteners on any boys who came round ar gaff.

'It was a lovely idea to meet here,' I said, nervously turning my attention to Giles' arl Fella, realising he was a much safer option. 'Although I did think we were meeting at

111

your place on the Wirral when Giles picked me up at Woodside.'

'Is that what he told you?' David laughed. 'We haven't lived there for fifteen years.'

'Really?' I asked, kicking Giles under the table for being such a liar.

'No, we live on the Isle of Man these days.' David grinned, flashing that same dreamy smile ar Giles had. 'Tax purposes.'

'Does that make you Manx?' I said, nervously trying to lighten the mood. 'I hate United, me.'

'Actually, you would call us Gaels if we were natives.' Sandra announced, as if she was reading it from Wikipedia, but at least she was talking to me now.

Thankfully David found it funny, chipping in with a gag of his own. 'Although I'm sure Giles has told you, we've all been blue-noses since birth.'

Before I knew it, I was firing one back. The more nervous I felt, the more I tended to make stupid jokes, which usually resulted in me making a complete and utter arse of myself. 'So this is how the other half of Merseyside live?'

'Yeah, we're just like you lot, really,' David said. 'Only we tend to be a little bit better off, financially speaking.'

'And *ar* trophy cabinets are just like yours,' I replied. 'Only they tend to be full of silverware.'

'Oh, I love this one, Giles,' his *arl* Fella exclaimed. 'Where did you find her?'

'Would you believe it if I said the local Hospital?' Giles said, which sounded kind of odd, seeing as he usually called it the *ozzy*. 'I went for an X-ray after twisting my ankle and there she was. Couldn't keep her hands off me.'

'I was only doing my job,' I said. 'Although it was actually a bit of overtime. I usually work in the Intensive Care Unit.'

'Wow!' David said and I could tell he was genuinely impressed. 'With this virus going around, we're all about to realise just who the real heroes are. I for one have always thought you guys do a wonderful job, isn't that right Sandra?'

'Always,' she replied, barely looking up from her cocktail and I began to feel a bit sorry for her. Maybe English wasn't her first language because she spoke in this really *hard-to-place* accent, or perhaps she was just one of those down-trodden women whose husbands spoke for them.

Thankfully, with the help of a couple of Pinot Grigios, I made it through the main course, without making a total arse of myself. David and I were getting on famously, firing banter back and forth, but I still couldn't get a proper conversation out of Sandra. So imagine my horror as she offered to join us, when I excused myself to use the ladies. It was one thing having a natter with the *gerls* in the *clossit*, when we were on a night out, but this was going to be a whole new world of awkwardness.

'Sorry, I haven't said much at the table,' Sandra said, as she started applying her *lippy* in the mirror next to me. 'It's not you luv, honest.'

'Well, that's a relief,' I said, still feeling a little guarded.

'It was ar Giles' last girlfriend, if you must know,' she said. 'Ar David insisted he went to the best college and university, but you should've seen this *Judy* he brought back in his final year. Amelia something or other. Proper stuck up her own arse she was. Thought she was so much better than us lot. And guess what?'

'What?' I said, realising by now there was no problem with Sandra's English, she'd just been trying to hide her scouse accent.

'Despite her elocution lessons and all that, it was her arl Fella's business that was really going South,' she said triumphantly. 'Part of me wonders if she was only interested in ar Giles for his money.'

'Sounds horrible,' I said.

'She was,' Sandra replied. 'I'm sure Giles has told you all about her.'

'Not a word,' I said, 'It seems there's a few things he might've forgotten to mention. Like you guys living on the Isle of Man.'

'Oh don't be like that,' Sandra said. 'I'm sure he was just a little wary about meeting another gold digger. It can't be easy for him, with ar David finally making it onto the *Times Rich List*.'

'I can only imagine,' I said, a little bit lost for words if I was honest. 'Although, not that I'd know much about that, coming from a council house in Tockie.'

'*Shurrup!*' Sandra screamed. 'Where abouts?'

'Aspen Grove?' I said, nervously.

'Vandyke!' she replied.

'Oh my god,' I said. 'What a small world.'

'Isn't it?' Sandra laughed. 'Those were the days. I used to love ar summer holidays over at Southport. Which reminds me, *ar* Giles did tell you to bring your *bayden cossie*, didn't he? The spa treatments here are to die for.'

'Nah, it must've been another one of those things which slipped his mind,' I said, still reeling from the revelations about this mysterious ex-girlfriend and the fact his arl Fella was probably worth more than Paul McCartney.

'I'd let you borrow mine, seeing as I've got a horrible food baby going on at the minute and I'd rather not mess up me *'urr* do.' Sandra said, walking behind me and grabbing hold of both my breasts. 'But I'm not sure you get those puppies inside if I'm honest.'

Well, I was completely lost for words now.

'Are they real?' she asked, turning me around and forcefully placing my hand on hers. 'If I'd had a pair like that I'd never have got mine done.'

At this point it wasn't only my family's football team who played in red. My cheeks had turned that colour too.

'Thanks,' I muttered, unsure of what else to say.

'I bet ar Giles loves to get hold of them,' she said, finally letting my hands go. 'If he's anything like his arl Fella then he must be a boob man.'

'That's funny,' I said, stopping myself from going any further. It's just if my first impressions of David in the lobby were anything to go by, he was actually a bit of a bum man too.

'Between you and me, he is alright in the bedroom?' Sandra asked.

'What Giles?' I said, completely shocked by now.

'It's just you've got to watch these fly boys,' she added. 'They can be a little quick on the trigger, if you know what I mean.'

'All, good there,' I said. Although I did realise, I might not be able to look at ar Giles' arl Fella in quite the same light again.

Thankfully from there on, we got along famously. The four of us, laughing and joking ar way through a round of coffees and a stack of desserts. Although ar Giles did make me laff when he asked what we'd been up to in the ladies. 'You two were gone a long time,' he said, shooting a glance across the table towards his arl *gerl's* low-cut dress. 'She didn't end up showing you her tits did she?'

'Why is it, that every time us gerls go to the *clossit* together, you fellas always think we're looking at each other's breasts?' I said sternly, before smiling at Sandra.

'I know,' she giggled. 'Bloody disgraceful.'

I was really sad when we finally had to go. Apparently there was a limit to how many nights David and Sandra were allowed to stay on the mainland before they became liable for income tax. But if that wasn't surprising enough, I was even more shocked when I found how they were travelling back. Apparently, since handing much of the day to day running of the company over to ar Giles, David had only gone and got himself a pilot's license.

'Are you sure you don't want a ride on my chopper,' he joked, as I kissed him goodbye.

'Maybe next time,' I laughed, noticing his hand had dropped a little low again as he kissed us goodbye.

'Oh for God's sake don't encourage him,' Giles interrupted. 'He already thinks he's James Bond.'

It was almost dark when we finally got back in the car and started making ar way up the motorway. By now I was absolutely shattered. The mixture of all that food and wine and the gentle hum of the engine slowly sent me drowsy. So I lent my head against Giles' shoulder as he drove. He had the radio on playing some mushy romantic music and, despite the fact we'd been out all day, I could still smell the faintest hint of his aftershave. It was comforting. A subtle blend of citrus fruits. Although in the past few weeks it had become more than that. It had started to smell like home. If I knew then what was waiting for us just around the corner, I might've asked him what brand it was. But instead, I was fighting the urge to confront him about this ex-girlfriend who hurt him so badly, or why he hadn't been more open about his parents living on the Isle of Man. I guess his Ma was right. He was just wary of being hurt again, so I let it rest. I didn't want to ruin an otherwise perfect moment.

I think I'd actually drifted off to sleep when my phone rang, disturbing me with a start. At first I wondered if it was Ma. Although she'd insisted I still go on this date with Giles, we had agreed she'd call me if there was any news about the arl Fella. So I was a little surprised when it turned out to be Richie.

'Hey, Lozzle. It's me,' he said, far too excited to be the bearer of bad news. 'I know you're out with Giles but I need you back here pronto.'

'Oh my God. Has the *auld* man woken up?'

'Not yet,' he said. 'They're slowly lowering his dose of sedatives. It might be tomorrow, but it's more likely to be Monday now. Me and Wayne went round this afternoon.'

'Together?' I asked.

'Yes, together,' Richie replied. 'What's wrong with that?'

'Nothing,' I replied. 'Just a little surprised, that's all.'

'Well, not as surprised as you're going to be when I tell you the news,' Richie said, mysteriously. 'So can you make it to the *Plaza* tonight?'

'Well, I'm not sure I can manage anymore to eat, I've been out with Giles' *auld* folks at some posh place in

119

Cheshire. But I could meet you for a drink,' I said. 'What's this all about anyway?'

'I'll tell you when you get here.' Richie replied, sternly. 'And bring the blue-nose if you want. It would be nice to meet him.'

By now he'd got me properly intrigued, so I had no choice but to go. I had been absolutely dreading this moment. Introducing ar Giles to my brothers. It wasn't just the Everton and Liverpool rivalry, or the fact they'd chased away all my boyfriends when I was young. It was a class issue. I wasn't so worried about ar Richie, after all he could hold his own with anyone in the business stakes. It was ar Wayne. I wasn't ashamed of him. He was a total sweetie and he had a real heart of gold when he was sober. Just that wasn't very often. It very much depended on which Wayne showed up. That's all. And none of us could ever really predict that.

Having said all that, after meeting ar Giles' family I suddenly didn't feel quite so worried. David was probably the most down to earth millionaire you could ever wish to meet and, as for his Sandra, well, she was a *Tockie* from Vandyke. Although I realised it was best not to mention that, seeing as she was a similar age to ar Wayne and Richie. They might have known each other, even dated. Or worse. *Swerve that.*

As we arrived at the Plaza I'd just about prepared myself. I'd even given Richie another ring to let him know we were here and to enquire about ar Wayne's sobriety. 'Everything's fine,' he said.

So imagine my horror when I saw them both looking like a couple of football hooligans standing at the bar. It was hard to tell whether Wayne had been injured, after all, his face was always a bit puffy with the alcohol. But ar Richie had a definite shiner under one eye and some home-made butterfly stitches taped above the other. 'Oh please don't tell me you've been fighting again,' I said

'Indeed we have,' ar Wayne replied, surprisingly sober but reeking of fags. 'But not with each other this time.'

'Oh,' I said, a little bit shocked. 'And there was me thinking you'd been to the *ozzy* to see the arl Fella.'

'We did,' Richie said, slapping ar Wayne hard across the back. 'We just bumped into a couple of *blert*s along the way, who ended up messing with the wrong brothers.'

'I suppose that's all right, then.' I said, incredibly confused, but at least kind of pleased they were getting on. 'Giles, I'm really sorry to say these two *meffs* are my brothers, Richie and Wayne.'

'Don't let ar Richie give you any hassle,' Wayne said, jumping in first and holding out his hand. 'Or I'll sort him out for you.'

'Yeah, but he'll probably let me get a couple of light ones in first.' Richie laughed, as he came around the side and pretended to rough Giles up. 'After all, you are a bloody blue nose, aren't you?'

To be fair, Giles took it pretty well. 'So let me get this straight, you're Wayne and this is Richie?'

I knew what he was getting at. After all, I had described them on numerous occasions as the *sensible one* and the *crazy one*. Standing there looking at them, it was hard to tell which one was which. 'So what's this all about?' I asked, as we all took a seat. 'Mags is not screwing you over for your apartment in this divorce case is she?'

'I'm afraid she is,' Richie replied. 'But that's not it.'

'Bloody money grabbing bitch,' I said, turning towards ar Giles. 'Sorry, luv.'

'Sorry for what?' he asked and I realised I'd come dangerously close to letting slip what me and his arl gerl had really been discussing in the ladies earlier. Thankfully he didn't seem to pick up on it. 'Look it's great to meet you both at last,' he said. 'Would you mind if I got the bill tonight?'

'Nope, it's my treat,' Wayne said. 'I had a bit of luck on the gee-gees today.'

'Oh, my Dad's got a couple of horses. Where do you keep yours?' Giles asked, obviously confusing him for the sensible one.

'Ladbrokes, mostly,' Wayne said. 'But occasionally I go to Betfred.'

Honestly I could've died. 'Can you just get on with this?' I asked, turning to Richie.

'Well, do you remember that girl ar Kenny used to knock about with in his last year at school,' he stuttered. 'Sorry, of course you don't. You weren't even born.'

'Oh, I remember,' Wayne said. 'She looked like Sinita, but spoke like Carol Decker. I would've shagged the arse of that.'

'Thanks for that,' I said, returning my attention to ar Giles. 'There's nothing like a bit of objectification of women to lighten the mood.'

'Honestly, don't worry,' Giles said. 'I've heard worse.'

'Anyway, Lauren,' Richie continued, only now I knew it was serious because he never called me Lauren. 'I met her daughter earlier this week. She's thirty.'

'What are you trying to say, Rich?' I asked, although I already feared where this was heading.

He scrolled through the pictures on his phone before handing it to me. 'Once you get over the initial likeness to her mother, you can't tell me there isn't something in her eyes that doesn't remind you of ar Kenny.'

'She doesn't look anything like him,' I said, adamantly. Although truth be told I'd only ever seen him in photographs.

'You're only saying that because she's black,' Wayne said, peering over my shoulder.

'*Shurrup* up Wayne,' I snapped, although to be honest, I was just relieved he hadn't used some vile, outdated racist slur. 'So what are you suggesting Richie, that we invite her round for Sunday dinner and introduce her to Ma as her long lost granddaughter?'

'Well, I wasn't going to go that far until we get a paternity test,' Richie said, taking back his phone. 'But she could come along tomorrow as my guest, just to set the ball rolling.'

'Last I heard you hadn't even told Ma about your divorce,' I said. 'How are you going to explain that you're bringing along a thirty year-old *gerl* as your guest.'

'I could tell Ma she's a client,' Richie said. 'Which is not entirely a lie. I am thinking about calling Vicky Jepson who manages Liverpool ladies about her. You should see her play. A proper chip off the old block.'

'A chip off the block?' Wayne interjected. 'You couldn't catch a pig in a jigger.'

'Not me,' Rich said. 'Ar Kenny. She's a centre-forward and everything.'

'No,' I said, coming between them. 'It's not happening. Why can't you just wait until you've had the paternity test and the arl Fella is out of the *ozzy*.'

'I'll be gone by then,' Richie said. 'I'm only here for another week then it's off to Argentina. I've got a prospective client over there who I'm trying to tie down to a deal before the Copa América.'

'Nice one, Richie.' I said, suddenly sounding like ar Wayne. 'So you want to parachute in here, fix all ar family worries in a fortnight and disappear into the sunset.'

'That's hardly fair,' Richie said.

'Isn't it?' I asked, turning to Wayne for support.

'Don't get me involved.' He shrugged.

'A bloody whacker isn't that what you usually call him?' I shouted, but now I realised we really had come full circle. There I was rowing with Richie and ar Wayne was the one trying not to take sides. It was like the bloody twilight zone.

'That's enough,' Giles said, standing up behind my chair and ushering me away. 'I think we've all had enough for tonight.'

125

So, that's how my day ended, being dragged out the *Plaza* like a feral cat. And all I could think about was poor Giles. What must he have thought about ar family. One thing's for sure. It was a million miles away from the *Times Rich List*, hotels in Cheshire and the *Isle of bloody Man*.

Chapter 13
Lauren Kennedy
15th March 2020

I was already awake when Ma returned from the *ozzy*, having spent another night sleeping at the arl Fella's bedside. Whilst I tried to talk her out of it, she insisted on cooking one of her world famous roasts, which we'd all nicked-named the *bollockathon*, due to the fact there was so much food, we had to *bollock* it all into us in order to get through it. Today was clearly no exception. She was only half-way through the prep and there was already going to be enough to feed an entire football team.

Just like yesterday's derby, I hoped ar Sunday lunch might yet be cancelled. It's not that I was praying for more coronavirus related disruptions, but Ma had already left me strict instructions of what to do, should the arl Fella wake up. She was going to drop everything to return to his bedside and I was going to finish serving up. Whilst I wasn't really in the mood to wait on either of my two brothers, finishing off a half-baked dinner seemed a vastly better option to participating in ar Richie's half-baked plan of inviting a mysterious guest to dinner, only to forget to mention she might be ar Kenny's long-lost daughter.

Before long Ma was cheerfully singing away from the kitchen and I was relegated to the lounge to listen out for the phone. I realised it was doing her good, having something to take her mind off the waiting. There I was, left to contemplate the disaster of last night's dinner. It was always my plan to invite Giles over today, but we both agreed when he dropped me off that it was probably best to leave it for another weekend. He still hadn't actually met my Ma and, whilst neither of us wanted to make a massive deal out of it, we didn't want it to end up being a support act to Richie's little freak show. I was just glad he was still replying to my texts.

I knew ar Richie meant well, but I couldn't understand why he didn't get it. This wasn't like opening a can of vegetables, it was like opening Pandora's box. This type of thing required both time and planning. Not just for Ma and the arl Fella, but for this girl, Amber, too. Even if we were all related, it didn't instantly make us a family. It would probably require some level of counselling for everyone to get used to the idea. But I suppose it was typical Richie. He always did throw himself headlong into things. At first it had been University, where he got his Law degree, and then it was his career. Maybe he wasn't so different to ar Wayne after all. Only his addiction was work.

I was still hoping for a last minute reprieve when the doorbell eventually rang. Running down the hallway, I tried to get there first, praying I could talk ar Richie out of it. But Ma beat me to it. Standing there in her scruffy apron, she threw her arms around Richie and Wayne, before looking more than a little embarrassed when she realised ar Richie had brought a guest.

'Hi, Ma,' Richie said. 'This is Amber, I hope you don't mind feeding one more. She's a potential new client of mine and I thought one of your roast dinners might help seal the deal.'

'Of course not. Sit yourselves down and I'll go and change.' Ma said, waiting for them to walk past into the back kitchen before grabbing my arm. 'If that's his new client then call me a blue-nose,' she said. 'No offence. But I knew he was having problems with his marriage.'

Well, I didn't know what to say, but as I went to join them at the table, I realised keeping the truth away from Ma was going to be much harder than any of us first thought. 'So, Amber,' I said, trying to sound her out, before Ma returned. 'How old did you say you were?'

'I didn't,' she replied.

'Well, I'm thirty later this year,' I added. 'So I guess that makes us about the same age, doesn't it?'

'Give or take a year,' Amber said, and I began to wonder whether she wanted to be a part of this either.

'So what school did you go to?' I continued, hoping we could settle this before Ma came down.

Amber fidgeted nervously. 'Saint Hilda's followed by Bellerive.'

'Oh, I went to Bellerive,' I said. 'Who was your form teacher?'

'Mrs Hodge,' Amber stuttered. 'Did you know her?'

'Nope,' I said, confidently. 'What year did you say it was?'

'I don't know. Late nineties,' Amber replied, desperately looking across to Richie for support.

'Well, I was there from two thousand and one, until two thousand and six and there was no Mrs Hodge,' I said, with absolute certainty.

'What at Bellerive Catholic School?' Amber asked.

'Oh no,' I said, suddenly realising there were two Bellerive Schools. 'I went to the secular School across the road. My arl Fella was a Lutheran Minister and they didn't have a school of their own.'

'Is that right?' Amber said, clearly looking relieved.

'Are you satisfied now?' Richie interjected, in a slightly threatening tone. 'What is this, a bloody interrogation?'

'Am I satisfied?' I asked and I was just about to give him a proper action replay of last night's dinner when Ma came down, looking lovely in a floral blouse and a long flowing skirt.

'Is everything alright?' she said.

'Everything looks lovely, Mrs Kennedy,' Amber said, politely.

'Please, call me Susan,' Ma said.

I helped Ma serve up and we made ar way through the main course, keeping the conversation to a minimum. Of course Ma asked why ar Richie looked like he'd been beaten up. I could see she wasn't buying the story that he'd slipped in the shower. 'What are you eighty-four?' she joked. 'Why do I get the feeling you are all keeping something from me.'

We all looked dead nervous until ar Wayne piped up.

'Before we get started on dessert, there's something I want to tell you,' he said, having been remarkably quiet until then.

I looked across at Richie, before kicking ar Wayne hard beneath the table. 'Don't you dare.'

He pulled out a couple of photographs from his pocket and passed them down towards Ma. 'Look what ar Lozzle found when she was cleaning my flat.'

I held my hands up to apologise. To be honest if he wasn't sitting across the table, I could've thrown my arms around him. Like me, he obviously realised this wasn't a good idea and he was doing his best to run some interference.

Ma looked at the *auld* photo of her and the arl Fella and said tearfully, 'This is lovely Wayne. Can I keep it?'

'Of course,' Wayne said. 'We even found that picture Lozzle drew of ar Kenny on her fifth birthday. You know that one when he looked all pale, with those blacked-out eyes.'

By now I wondered if hc had gone too far.

'Shurrup,' Ma replied, suddenly smiling. 'Pissed all over your Nan's trifle that did. God rest her soul.'

'He was meant to be a clown,' I said, grinning a little sheepishly. 'That's how I pictured him growing up.'

By now Ma just started laughing. 'There was this one time when we all went to Pontins in Blackpool,' she said. 'I dressed ar Kenny up as a clown for the fancy dress. Only I'd got the wrong night. It was the adult's fancy dress competition, poor little lamb.'

'I remember that,' Wayne said, pissing himself now too. 'But none of the grown-ups bothered taking part, so he still ended up winning. The compere kept trying to ask him why he should win, obviously referring to the fact nobody else was dressed up.'

'Oh yeah, and ar Kenny just kept saying, it's because I'm the best!' ar Richie added.

'Had me and your arl Fella in stitches, that one,' Ma said, a little teary-eyed. 'But they gave him a tonne of stuff to make up for the embarrassment.'

'Was that the holiday we broke down on the seafront just as we arrived, Ma?' Richie asked.

'Oh yeah,' Wayne chuckled. 'In that awful beige Austin Allegro with the brown roof and the dodgy head-gasket.'

'Whatever happened to that?' Richie asked.

By now ar Ma was in hysterics. 'Oh you must remember that. The baboons at Knowsley Safari Park finally finished it off. They tore the bloody roof to shreds and dry humped the aerial off the back. The bloody randy buggers.'

Even though it was well before my time, it was lovely to watch them. *Laffing* about the auld days. 'Well you learn something every day don't you?' I said. 'Maybe that's why I saw Kenny as a clown growing up?'

'Maybe,' Wayne said, grinning mischievously. 'Hey Rich, isn't that the holiday you got stung by a bee on the beach.'

'Yes,' he said, burying his head in his hands, as if he already knew where this was headed.

133

'Then you stood up and cried for somebody to call the *bizzies*.' He laughed. 'Me and Kenny gave you proper stick for that one. We ended up calling you *bizzie the bee*.'

Even though I'd never actually met him, I think we could all pretty much picture ar Kenny by now. Even Amber. I had the feeling we'd all developed ar own image of him over the years, but suddenly, it was like he was actually sat at the table with us. Not only that, but just for a second, there was none of the hurt. We were all laughing and joking. Maybe there really was something to this story with Amber. I knew it sounded crazy, but maybe, just maybe she'd brought Kenny's spirit with her.

I looked across at Richie and I could see he was thinking it too. I knew it was risky, but there probably wasn't going to be a better chance. 'Ma, there's something Richie wants to tell you.'

But just then, the phone rang. '*Gissus* a minute, luv.' Ma went into the front room and picked it up, leaving the door open a crack, so we could just about hear what she was saying. She didn't say a lot. There was some tutting, a couple of, 'Oh, I sees,' and one, 'Are you sure?' Then she returned, white as a sheet and cleared her throat. 'Kids, it's your arl Fella,' she said and I could tell it was going to be bad news.

'Please don't say it, Ma.' I cried. I just thought if she didn't say it, then it couldn't be true.

'Is he dead?' Wayne asked, his bottom lip trembling.

Richie stood up and went over to console her.

'Nope,' Ma said, suddenly taking control of herself. 'He's tested positive for that blasted virus, so they're keeping him sedated a while longer.'

Chapter 14
Susan Kennedy
15th March 2020

I must have sat there all night in the kitchen. Long after Richie and Wayne had left, long after Lauren had gone to bed. Of course they'd offered to sit up with us, but I'd forced them away. Lauren was back to work in the morning and Richie had brought some strange guest with him, which he claimed was one of his clients. Of course I didn't believe him. All I really wanted was to go and see my Ezzy, but the nurse had been quite adamant it wouldn't be possible over the phone. Apparently it wasn't safe.

I was sixteen years-old when I first laid eyes on him. Back then, home wasn't my favourite place. My arl Fella was a good man, but nobody could live up to his impossible standards, least of all him. There were days when he took out his own short-comings on me and Ma. We were often shouted at to clean the floor or fold his dirty linen. On my bedroom wall I was only allowed two posters. One was the fifth Beatle, Georgie Best, despite being a Liverpool fan I really fancied him. The other was a little known rhythm and blues singer at the time by the name of Van Morrison. Everybody I knew was into the Beatles back then. Sure they were fine if you liked that sort of thing, but they were a bit too clean-cut in the early days and far too like the local lads if you asked me. Give me a Northern Irish accent any day of the week. The moment I heard him speak I was wet through.

That Belfast boy had a look of *Georgie boy* and the speaking voice of *Van the Man*. He could've talked the knickers of her *Maj*, given half the chance. He was working down the docks *where the bugs wore clogs* when we first locked eyes. To this day, I can't remember what I was doing there, but in that moment, something changed. He was singing along to an *auld* transistor radio, which he used to carry around as he worked. Although he could barely carry a tune, I must have stopped and drooled because of his accent. I think he'd only mentioned that I'd got a lovely pair of eyes and he wanted to take me out on Friday and I was already his *gerl*. Even knowing what I knew now, I wouldn't have changed a thing. Although knowing ar Ezzy like I did now, he probably meant I had a lovely pair of legs and that he wanted to do a lot more than just take me out.

I must admit, I sometimes found it hard to understand him. Like when he'd asked me to the pictures the following week. I did wonder whether Liverpool had a cup match against Fulham that night, by the way he over pronounced the letter 'l' in the word film. Still, I'll never forget that magical evening. We watched *Who's Afraid of Virginia Woolf* at the

Madge and danced the night away down the *Ippy*. From that moment on, he called me his *Brown-Eyed Girl* and it soon became ar song. I was working as a stock-girl at the Bemrose Printers at the time and I just couldn't wait to get off work every Friday. Partly because my boss was a bit of a letch. I remember him telling me to stand on a fork-lift truck in my Mary Quant mini-skirt and then asking the driver to raise me up so everybody on the shop floor could have a butchers at my underwear. But I just laughed it off. You did in those days. For me it didn't matter because I just couldn't wait to get out of there and get down the docks to listen to my favourite songs with ar Ezzy on his *auld* radio.

Later that winter, we spent three months apart, when he went back home to see his arl Fella before he died of cancer. He had worried if I'd wait for him. But he needn't have bothered. I walked past the docks every day, practically pining. On the day of his return, I got there three hours early, just so I could hear that fog horn blow. Just like that other Van Morrison song we both liked, I couldn't wait for him to rock my gypsy soul. I just wanted to hear his gruff Irish accent. Like broken glass dipped in honey. Even though he was already a man of faith, that Irish boy knew more than just how to talk. He had the moves. Oh boy, did he have the moves, just thinking about it makes me blush.

I would've married him there and then, but things became a bit tight with him losing his apprenticeship. To be honest it was never really his calling, he just followed in his arl Fella's footsteps. His *auld* man had worked night and day at Harland & Wolfe in Belfast, the same mighty shipyard where they built the Titanic, although that was a little before his time. By a strange twist of fate, his Grandfather had forged the steel which formed the hull of that stricken vessel, in a foundry across the water in Motherwell. But as ar Ezzy would've said, that was so long ago, Jesus was still playing full-back for Israel.

Ezzy's apprenticeship is what brought him over from Belfast, but times had changed. Shipping and steel were in decline. Harland and Wolfe were consolidating their position and moving back across the water and ar Ezzy wasn't going with them. It was about then he told me of his plans to become a Minister. It's how he went from being a Protestant to a Lutheran, almost overnight. It's pretty much the same thing, he said, only they follow the teachings of a preacher called Martin Luther. Not to be confused with the civil rights activist, Martin Luther-King, like I had done, when he first explained it to me. All in all, he cared little for the subtle differences in liturgical practices. All he knew is the world which contained his brown-eyed girl was far too beautiful to be an accident, therefore, someone must've created it. That someone was God and he was going to spend the rest of his days playing for his team, even if they didn't play in red. Although Ezzy was pretty sure they did.

Like I said, he was a smooth talker ar Ezzy.

So we lived in sin. Quite something in those days and, my God, did we sin. Morning, noon and night. He was as randy as a butcher's dog that one, we both were. I love my children, but in many ways, they were the best years of my life. Of course when I fell pregnant in the spring of seventy-one, he finally made an honest woman out of me. About bloody time too. I had my eye on a bridal gown from Clayton Square, but we couldn't stretch that far and they wouldn't have had enough material to stretch it over my growing bump anyway. So my arl *Gerl* made me one just like it. She walked me down the aisle too, my bully of an arl Fella had passed away by then. Other than that, we kept it traditional on the way down, but we came back up the aisle to *Stuck in the Middle With You,* by *Stealers Wheel.* It was my idea not Ezzy's. Originally he thought it was a play on words relating to his Grandfather's days in the steel industry, but it was that line in the chorus I'd fallen in love with. *Clowns to the left of me, jokers to the right.* I think everyone in the church laughed at that moment, including ar *Ezzy.* Despite those ocean-coloured eyes and the fact he was sporting a bushy beard by then, he was far more like James Dean than the accepted image of Jesus. Although he was more of a *rebel with a cause,* of helping people, than the hopeless drifter from the movie.

In the space of three years, we bagged a hat-trick, with three beautiful baby boys. Despite the constant patter of tiny feet, that dirty bugger from across the water couldn't keep his hands to himself. Neither could I. At one point we planned to start ar own football team. Maybe we would've done too, if it hadn't been for ar Richie. He tried hard, but he couldn't catch a pig in a jigger that one. You couldn't even stick him in goal because the ball would always end up going between his legs. For a while it looked like ar Wayne was the pick of the litter. He was an awesome right-winger. But he had a right temper too and when a Liverpool scout came to watch him, he got himself sent off. All was not lost. He actually noticed ar Kenny that afternoon. With him being one year younger, he was always the smallest on the pitch. With his oversized shirt and his shorts held up with a bootlace, we'd got bigger candles on the altar. We used to make him play in Wayne's team because they put two years together back then. Seeing as most of the matches were on a Sunday and ar Ezzy was at church, there was only me to take them. It was the only way

for both of them to get a game, with ar Richie always happier
watching, with his head buried in some *bewk* taking notes.
The following year, Wayne remained on the side-lines too,
mostly through choice, but he had racked up a six-match
suspension. Finally ar Kenny got to play with kids his own
size instead of moving up.

That's when he began to shine. He had his arl Fella's thick
black hair. So I didn't have to perm it, which was all the rage
back then. He played centre forward, and he looked like
Kevin Keegan. Played like him too, only better. He scored
sixty-two that season, beating Dixie Dean's record and
everything. I must admit, I only got into football for the boys,
but I'd come to love it by then. Shouting "Hit him *wid yer
'andbag*," every time a tackle came in too timid or "*Buy a
bewk ref*," every time a decision went against us. I was
always on the touchline Sunday afternoons, wind, rain or
shine. But I allowed ar Ezzy the honour to take them to
Anfield on Saturdays, opting to stay at home. It's not that I
didn't want to go. I'd really gotten into it by then. It's just
footy on a Saturday was father and son time, and I owed
Ezzy that much.

What happened next you've probably read about in the
newspapers. If you haven't then I guess it was like the

moment ar Ezzy took us to watch Titanic and they hit the iceberg. I cried out, "No!" And grabbed hold of his arm tightly. All he could say was, "As if you didn't know that was going to come?"

Of course I knew it was coming. I was just enjoying all the finery and splendour of that ship they'd recreated and I wanted to savour it a bit longer.

Well, my Titanic happened on 15th April nineteen-eighty nine, in the FA Cup semi-final between Liverpool and Nottingham Forest. I hadn't even wanted them to go to Hillsborough, it was too far to travel in my opinion and they never went away. But Sheffield had been chosen because it apparently had good transport links to Liverpool and it was big enough to withstand the crowd. Or so they thought, just like that ill-fated ship which set sail from Southampton all those years earlier.

The first mistake they made was allocating ar fans the smaller end of the stadium, despite being the bigger club. Then, shortly before kick-off, in an attempt to ease overcrowding outside the entrance, the Police Commander ordered they open an extra gate, leading to a wave of supporters into the *Leppings Lane Stand*. It was an old-fashioned standing-only terrace, like most grounds at the time. They seemed to have no regard for how many people it

144

could actually hold and this led to a crush of supporters entering the stadium.

It was only five minutes past three, when the ref blew the whistle to halt play, but it was already too late. By then people were already scaling the fences, trying to escape. Despite there being hundreds of Police on duty, the players were the first to react. I can still remember Bruce Grobbelaar stewarding people to safety. He was often seen as a crazy figure standing in the Liverpool goal. Coming out to claim crosses one-handed, or wobbling his knees together when the opposition had a penalty. Despite that, he was the greatest keeper ever to wear the number one jersey at Liverpool, a real safe pair of hands. Sadly for me, even Bruce Almighty's hands were not infallible that day.

In the following weeks police fed stories to the press, suggesting hooliganism and drunkenness by Liverpool supporters had caused the disaster. The blaming of Liverpool fans persisted even after the first inquiry in nineteen eighty-nine. The *Taylor Report*. What a load of shite that turned out to be. The first coroner's inquest a year later ruled that every single one of those deaths was accidental. Ninety-six families torn apart and an accident was the best they could come up with. Not only that, they were blaming the fans for their own deaths. Well, I for one wasn't having it.

The next few years were a bit of a blur. I can't remember much, although ar Ezzy was always by my side. That sweet talking Preacher man still had his moments and that must have been when we made ar Lauren, or Lozzle as we call her now. I remember her drawing this awful picture of Kenny on her fifth birthday. It pretty much ruined the day for me, but other than that she was an absolute cherub.

There must've been times when I neglected her. I just couldn't understand why these enquiries and coroners couldn't get it into their thick skulls. It wasn't an accident. We hadn't lost something we could just replace. There wasn't a day went by which I didn't think about my son. Even on my daughter's birthday, he was ever present. I even saw him sometimes. Usually, he'd appear as an angelic altar boy singing at church with his arl Fella. Which is ironic because it's me who pulled him out of the choir to play centre forward for *Tockie*. I suppose I didn't want to remember him as the Keegan-haired centre forward, who was all set for the big-time. It was just too painful.

So I joined the fight, every group and every panel which would have me and even ones which wouldn't. From that day on, I only had one thing on my mind. Justice. Whatever that meant. If I'm honest, I'm still not sure now.

Ar Ezzy, having a direct line to the big man upstairs, somehow found the courage to continue. He still managed to stand up in front of those people at church every Sunday and listen to their worries. When all the while, his suffering was far greater than any of theirs. For that I admired him even more than I did for his Georgie Best good-looks and his voice like broken glass, which never lost its Tupelo honey. I just wished I'd told him all of that before his stroke.

We slowly drifted apart over the next thirty years. I spent my days fighting and he spent his time on his allotment. He was still a great father. But he wasn't always present as a husband. And I filled those two great holes left in my life by gunning for the bastards. I fought them every inch of the way.

It turned out there was much more to it than a mere accident. An accident is when you step on someone's foot on the bus and you say sorry before you both move on. This was different. Firstly, it wasn't the first time they'd hosted a semi-final at Hillsborough. A similar incident had occurred at the Leppings Lane Stand during the nineteen eighty-one semi-final, between Tottenham and Wolves. On that day, the police had been commended for acting swiftly and I'll give them their due. After all, if they stopped just one mother going through what I did, then I'd happily have bought them all a round of drinks. But lessons hadn't been learned. Why were there still *standing-only* terraces and why wasn't there a way to count how many fans were being allowed in each stand?

Apparently, after that game, the Sheffield Wednesday chairman said there was no need to reduce the capacity, "It's not like somebody could've been killed," he said. Well, trust me, he might've been if I'd have got my hands on him. And I wasn't the only one. It seems their stadium had been deemed too small for such games for the next seven years. *So why did they bring it back again in eighty-nine?*

Then there were the trains. I discovered during the Sheffield Wednesday against Liverpool fixture earlier in the season, three trains had been scheduled to spread the arrival of the fans. During that fateful day, when my boys went, only one was chartered, causing all the fans to arrive together. There's no doubt this played a part in the initial surge outside the Leppings Lane Stand, which in turn led to the floodgates being opened.

And then there was this Police Commander. Now, I must be careful what I say here. But let's just say he was new to the job. A little wet behind the ears to be handling a game of this stature. Apparently, he'd never even had any training. By now I was convinced there was no bloody accident on that day. Sure it was tragic. But an accident suggests nobody was to blame. You couldn't say that about Hillsborough and you couldn't tell that to a mother who'd lost her son.

So I fought on and on. I forget just how many hearings I went to. I've still got the notes in lever arch files, dated and catalogued in ar loft. Some things have changed for the better, I'll grant you that. It won't bring back my boy, but it might prevent it happening again. Stadiums are all-seater these days and matches are controlled by better trained Commanders. But to me, and the others like me, it's like locking the gate after the horse has bolted.

In the final hearing last year, they found one person guilty of a minor health and safety breach, but the rest walked free. Many of them had not even been ordered to stand up in the dock. To say it was a travesty, was to say nothing at all, but now thirty years had passed. Thirty years since the Titanic crashed its way through my family and my marriage and left a giant hole in its wake. I lost a son and a husband that day. And ar Wayne was never right afterwards, either.

I think that final hearing led to ar Ezzy's stroke too. Behind the "Turn the other cheeks" and the "Let it go Susans," he'd been fighting alongside me all the way. And now it was too late. Too late to tell him how it wasn't his fault. Too late to tell him I forgave him anyway and too late

149

to tell him he was the love of my life and he could still rock my gypsy soul any day of the week.

And that's exactly what I needed to say to him.

Chapter 15
Ezra Kennedy
15th March 2020

I was having one of my dreams again, the sort you know is a dream, but you can't quite wake up. There I was, at Stanley Docks, strolling down the streets by the quayside. A golden sun sat low on the horizon, caressing everything in its gaze with the sentimental glow of a sepia-tone photograph. Brick-built buildings, which I knew should've been weathered and grey, seemed polished and pristine. Sat alongside them was a giant ship, but something wasn't right. Her black steel hull was pockmarked with rust, like she'd spent a lifetime at the bottom of the ocean. A string of fairy lights, caked in seaweed, hung loosely from her chimneys and a skeleton of exposed wires sparked angrily across the sky. I wouldn't have taken another step towards her, if I hadn't seen my father calling me aboard. Suddenly, it all made sense.

Looking back for a moment, I caught sight of my Susan. I tried to beckon her to join me, but it was no longer possible. The streets had become awash with well-wishers, men in flat-caps dancing a merry jig, along with ladies in long, frilly gowns, followed by a convoy of baggage boys. It's then I realised my sons were amongst them. All three of them, still blessed with the exuberance of youth.

The closer we got the more crowded it became. Some guards appeared in the gangways, but they were far too few in number to make their presence felt. As the crowd began to surge, I took matters into my own hands, opening my arms and clutching my boys towards my chest, trying to keep them safe. But the crowd was like an ocean wave, with an energy of its own. A storm was brewing on the quayside and I started to wonder if we might tear that rickety old girl from her moorings. I wasn't the only one. Nerves and ropes began to fray. Voices were raised. Batons were drawn and it seemed only a matter of time before the crowd turned violent.

There was an almighty blast from a whistle and suddenly another door appeared to open on the lower deck. It was like a storm, which seemed destined to hit us, had suddenly passed overhead. Any fear or anger was replaced by sunlight racing through the clouds. As we made the last few steps towards our destination, I almost forgot how the ship had looked from a distance. Her sheer bulk instantly made her feel sturdy underfoot. No longer being shoved and harried from behind, I looked back and savoured one last glimpse of Liverpool, with my boys by my side. Of course, I hoped I might spot their mother at the quayside, but sadly she was nowhere to be seen.

The moment we stepped onboard the feeling of overcrowding returned. The warmth of bodies, the fog of breath in the air and the stale smell of sweat. We heard rumours of finely dressed gentleman, sipping tea on the upper decks, but our tickets didn't allow us that far. Not that we minded. It might've been a bit cramped down below, but this is where the real party was. These were our people, the ones who felt most grateful to be onboard. And they weren't afraid to show it. Voices and glasses were raised, as people exchanged gestures of good health. Fiddles were drawn and songs were sung, with dancing erupting in anything which resembled an open space.

We were making such a racket, we could hardly hear the mighty engines roar as we lumbered out of the harbour. But we could feel it. The old girl bobbed and weaved as she laboured across the waves. We were packed in so tight by then, it only added to the fun. The boys were too young to partake in the drinking, but we did get stuck into the dancing. Kenny and Wayne linked arms and spun each other around. Richie sat on my shoulders, whilst I did my best to sway from side to side without dropping him. I remember wondering what more could a man wish for; his boys by his side and tickets to the greatest show on Earth.

That wonderful journey was supposed to last a lifetime, but it ended far too soon. Five minutes and as many seconds to be precise. That's when we struck something with an almighty thud. An echo reverberated around us and the sound of shearing steel rose up through my feet. Even then, I knew the situation was serious. Richie slipped from my shoulders, but I managed to cushion his fall and took him by the hand. Wayne grabbed hold of my other arm, but ar Kenny just smiled and said, 'As if you didn't know that was coming?'

And then he disappeared.

Panic didn't set in straight away. Maybe some people were too polite to cause a scene, whilst others were perhaps too drunk to care. But all that changed the moment water started rushing in around our ankles. 'Kenny!' I shouted, but he was nowhere to be seen.

I took Wayne and Richie by the hands. Of course we tried to turn back and look for Kenny, but we could no longer choose which direction we walked. Stray limbs, like live eels, wrapped themselves around us. Holding onto us. Pretty soon they were holding us up.

With the water rising to my knees, I began to worry for my boys. They were so much smaller than me, it was only a matter of time before they'd be starved of oxygen. With all my strength I wrapped an arm under each of them and lifted them to my shoulders, readying myself for one last push should the water smother me.

Whilst the crowd was moving rapidly, I wondered where they were heading. Getting this many people onboard was hard enough. Getting them off whilst we were at sea would surely be impossible. That's when I caught sight of my father again. He was standing inside an opening in the bulkhead, beckoning me over. 'What about Kenny?' I yelled, but before I knew it, he was gone.

We surged through the doorway, which led up a narrow flight of stairs. Spilling out on deck, daylight burnt my eyes. Still, at least we finally got a chance to see those finely dressed gentlemen. Only now, the remnants of their tea party floated around our ankles. What happened next really surprised me. Instead of running off in all directions, like headless chickens, people worked together. Complete strangers stopped to offer us a hand, risking their lives for the exchange of a quick glance and a smile. I'd have stopped to help a few more myself, but I had my boys to think about. Every time we came to an obstacle, a ladder to climb, or a gap to breach, I let them go first. Only to follow closely, trying not to let them escape from view.

It was an arduous, sometimes treacherous journey, which began to feel like a climb. The boat was sinking faster at one end and we were heading against the slope. But thanks to the kindness of many strangers, who I knew we'd never meet again, we finally made it to the lifeboats. By then even the fiddlers had managed to join us. Having resigned themselves to be the last to leave, they continued to play. In many ways theirs was the biggest sacrifice of all, keeping the peace with their calming melody, as the rest of us patiently waited to be saved.

'It's women and children first,' the guard said, when we finally got to the front. 'But I'll let you accompany these two if their mother isn't present.'

'I can't,' I replied. 'I have another son left behind.'

'Okay, but it's your funeral,' the guard replied.

'Come with us,' Wayne said, pulling on my sleeve as he stepped on board the lifeboat.

'You know I can't,' I said, tearing myself away from him. 'Look after your brother won't you.'

'I don't need looking after,' Richie said. 'Let us come with you.'

'Well, I need you both to look after your mother,' I said, nodding to the guard to cut them loose.

I allowed myself a moment to watch their boat being lowered. But the second they touched down safely, I turned my back and started fighting my way through the crowd. It was hard going at first, like swimming against the tide. Those same people who had shown us such kindness a moment earlier were now grabbing hold of me, urging me to turn back.

I didn't have time to explain. 'Kenny!' I yelled. 'Kenny!'

The stern of the ship was still sinking faster than the bow and the tide began to turn. Fewer people were making their way towards me now. It started to work in my favour. Before long, I was more or less falling forward. I arrived at the bulkhead door without a moment to spare. A pair of guards had just forced it closed and one was now trying to lock it with a giant ring of keys. 'I need to get in there.' I screamed. 'My son's down there!'

'Nobody's getting in there,' the one guard said.

I'm ashamed to say I put my hands on him. I didn't strike him, but with all my might I shoved him out the way. He staggered back and took out his baton.

'Stop!' his mate yelled. 'I'll open her up. But I'm locking it again behind you.'

When he opened the door I realised it wasn't people they'd been fighting back. It was floodwater. It gushed out so hard, it almost swept me away. Still, there was no turning back now, so I waited for it to subside before I waded forward. It was probably waist height when I heard the door lock shut behind me. 'Kenny!' I shouted. 'Kenny!' But he was nowhere to be seen.

The deeper I went, the higher the water came. I started to measure my breathing, expanding my chest with short staccato breaths before exhaling. I remembered some documentary I'd watched about these women who dived for pearls. Apparently, they could hold their breath for several minutes by flooding their body with oxygen before they went under.

I'd just resigned myself to the inevitable, when I spotted a door off to my right. I ripped a fire-axe off the wall and went to work on it, but it was made from solid steel. Striking it was futile. Wedging the axe inside its circular handle, I finally managed to twist it half a turn. The door flung open and water surged forward, driving me back to my knees.

I stood up to see another door and the race was on before the water filled the narrow chamber. Again and again this happened, with me opening one door, only to be faced with another. Like I said, part of me knew this was a dream. All I was doing was burrowing deeper and deeper into my subconscious. But like the captain of the ship, I wasn't leaving until I found my boy.

Chapter 16
Wayne Kennedy
16th March 2020

As the radio alarm clock rang, I rubbed my eyes and read the date. It was precisely one day short of a month until the thirty-first anniversary of ar Kenny's death. But other than that, there was nothing extraordinary about it. *Sixteen, zero, three, twenty-twenty.* They were by no means a memorable set of numbers, but the events which followed meant this would undoubtedly become one of those dates which everyone remembered where they were, like the day Kennedy got shot or the day Diana died. If yesterday's bombshell about my ar Fella contracting coronavirus had rocked me to my very core, then this would probably do the same for the rest of the nation. The country had officially gone into lockdown. Everything but supermarkets and essential retailers were to be closed with immediate effect.

After listening to the end of the bulletin, I turned off the radio and *laffed*. I'm not sure why, probably because it beat crying. It was kind of ironic that after all of the struggle, I wouldn't be able to cash in my betting slip, which I was keeping under my pillow. Whilst I might have a golden ticket with enough money to pay off my debts, the Deli Mob were unlikely to receive furlough. That meant they would still be looking for me and I'd have to keep a low-profile until this whole thing blew over.

Still, in many ways I realised I was already a winner. After all, that betting slip had brought me much closer to ar Richie than I could've possibly imagined. Also, my benefits were likely to be unaffected by the unprecedented turn of events. Whilst many people were now losing their jobs, I was one step ahead of them. With so many applying for help all at once, they'd undoubtedly face an almighty struggle to get their claims processed. So I lay back on my bed and started to wonder what my arl Fella would do to help if he was still able to get up off his.

As I couldn't actually go to see the *auld* man, I decided to go somewhere I could feel close to him. It had been so long, I could hardly remember the way, but when I finally arrived at his allotment, I was relieved to see it had hardly changed. Willow fences, slightly on the piss, surrounding plots of earth and broken sheds with old tin roofs silently keeping *douse*. The biggest problem was working out which one was his, but when I found a Liverpool scarf tied around a rickety gate-post, I knew I'd struck gold. The place was a bit of a mess, so I began by clearing away some weeds and dry leaves. Before I knew it, I was knees deep in muck and filth. Even then, I realised there was something special about that soil. Maybe it was because my arl Fella had shed his own sweat and tears there. I remember how he used to say anything we put our hearts into, inevitably our souls followed. Suddenly, with that thought, I felt him by my side.

Once I'd cleared away the top-layer, I was amazed at what lay beneath. Below the surface were beetroot, broccoli, sprouts and cabbages. My arl Fella must've planted them in the winter. Now, the sprouts were no bigger than *cherrywobs* but some of those cabbages were as big as footballs. It didn't take long to work out what he would've done with them. So with a great deal of care and a fair bit of effort, I dug them out. The only thing I didn't touch was a lonely rosebush in the corner. It hadn't quite come into flower, but it had plenty of buds coming through. All except one solitary bloom, the brightest shade of red, the colour of Liverpool. I considered taking a cutting and giving it to my Ma right away, but I thought better of it. I don't know why. Despite my arl Fella's absence, it seemed to have flourished pretty well where it was, so I thought it best to leave it be.

With a pile of veg, what I really needed next was a basket. Rummaging around in the shed, the only one I could find was attached to the front of a rusty bicycle. Although I had to clear away a load of stuff to actually get to it, eventually I was able to set it free. One of the bigger items was this *antwacky* transistor radio, which surprised me even more when I discovered it actually worked. At first it just spat and crackled, but before long I had strangled a tune out of it. I decided it would make a far better gift for Ma than chopping down that rosebush, so I put it to one side. As I forced that bike loose I found something else, something even more precious inside its basket. In an *auld* wooden frame, with a jagged crack across the glass, was a picture of Toxteth Tigers Under-Sixteens. Neither Richie or I played that year. I was banned for six games and I guess we all know ar Richie couldn't catch a pig in a jigger. That was Kenny's season. He scored sixty-two that year and broke Dixie Dean's record and everything. Only it didn't count, seeing as it was only junior football. Still, it got the scouts interested. There's no doubt he would've made it into the big leagues, given one more season. He was the best centre-forward I'd ever seen.

I loaded what vegetables I could into the basket and wheeled the bicycle out of the allotments down an *auld* muddy lane. I couldn't ride it because the tyres were flat, but other than that, everything else looked pretty solid. Still, it took me a while to get it down to Ma's, squeaking and rattling as I went. It was a strange feeling, it should've been the middle of rush hour, horns blaring and cars carving each other up at the lights, but I seemed to be the only person about. I could tell Ma was up though, she had the lights on downstairs and I saw her through the kitchen window. I tapped on the glass on my way past and she greeted me at the door with a smile. 'What have you got there, luv?'

'Ar arl Fella's *auld* bicycle,' I said, leaning it up against the wall. 'And a few veggies from his allotment, do you want some?'

'To be honest, ar Richie has just popped down to the supermarket to get me a load, but I'm sure there'll be a tonne of people who will find themselves short. Why don't you try your arl Fella's church? They started a food bank yesterday. Ezzy would love that.'

Of course she was right. 'Well, at least take this,' I said, removing the *auld* transistor radio from the basket and handing it to her.

'Oh my days,' she said, with a tear in her eye. 'I didn't know he still had this. Does it work?'

I extended the aerial which wasn't easy, seeing as it had rusted up. Then I fiddled with the dials. 'That's funny, it worked back at the allotment.'

'Probably just needs some new batteries,' a voice said from behind me.

'Alright me arl *meff*,' I said, turning to see ar Richie lugging a big box of groceries from the boot of his flash motor. 'There's a load more if you want to help.'

I gave him a hand lifting it out of the car, but he wouldn't let me step inside. 'It's called social distancing Wayne, you better get used to it now.'

'What about you?' I asked. 'How come you're allowed in?'

'I'm moving in with Ma for a while,' Richie replied, pulling a phone from his pocket and offering it to me. 'But I've got you this.'

'What do I want this for?' I said, struggling to even turn it on.

'To keep in touch in case something happens to ar arl Fella. I can't always get you on your land-line.'

'Fair enough, my arl *meff*.' I said, finally getting the screen to light up.

'It's only an *auld* one, but it still works. I got you a new SIM card and the number is written on the back. I even topped it up for you.'

'Thanks, mate,' I said, suddenly getting the urge to hug him. It's strange, we probably hadn't hugged for over thirty years and only now when I wasn't allowed did I really want to.

I wheeled that rusty bicycle across town. There were a few more people about now, some of them wearing these strange masks. Don't get me wrong, I understood. After all, my arl Fella was the strongest man I knew and if he was stricken with that virus, then it could probably take anyone. But I had to laugh at the people alone in their own cars with one on. I wondered if they lay in bed on their own too, wearing a condom on their old chap, just in case.

I got to the church about mid-morning, but it felt like midday. Not only because I'd done so much already, but the sun was brutal. I must've looked like a right *meff* when I parked my bicycle in the bike rack and stepped inside, covered in mud and sweat. I must admit, with everything going on, I was surprised to find it open. But then again, I remembered my arl Fella working right through the *Winter of Our Discontent* in seventy-eight, saying people needed God's word more than ever that year.

I walked down the aisle with a strange sense that I was trespassing, after all, only God knew how long it had been since I set foot inside a church. 'Can I help you?' a voice said, from over my shoulder.

I would be lying if I said it didn't scare the shit out of me. But when I turned round, I realised it wasn't Jesus, after all. It was just the interim Minister who had been taking care of things in my arl Fella's absence. Not that I knew him, I just recognised his outfit. 'Wayne, isn't it?' he said. 'We haven't met, but you look just like your father.'

'Got it in one.' I said, although I had to admit it landed like a back-handed slap. I knew I had city miles on my clock from years of hard-living, but I was a good twenty years younger than the *auld* man. 'I've come to drop off some vegetables for your food bank.'

'That's great,' he replied, walking with me to the door, but keeping his distance at the same time. 'Let's see what you've got shall we?'

I was relieved to step back outside. Not just because of the sunshine, it's just I'd never felt happy in church, despite my arl Fella's profession. 'This is only the start of it to be honest,' I said, bringing him over to the bicycle. 'There's a load more.'

'Well, this will be enough for us, we're after non-perishables really,' he said, shaking his head. 'But do you have a phone on you?'

It seemed an odd question, and an even more peculiar coincidence, but it just so happened I did. 'Of course, who doesn't carry a phone around?' I said, trying to play it down, but part of me was already thinking how the arl Fella used to say the Lord moved in mysterious ways.

'It's just there's a *Facebook* page for local people in need due to coronavirus,' he said. 'I'm sure you could find a home for all Ezra's vegetables there. You could even deliver them if you could only get that bicycle repaired, I've probably got something outback to fix that if you give me a minute.'

'Oh, that's not necessary,' I said, but he'd already gone back inside.

Now, it took him a lot longer than a minute. I began to wonder if by *outback* he actually meant Australia, but when he returned, he was clutching a bicycle pump and a repair kit. 'Do you want me to do it for you?'

'You've done enough,' I replied, desperate to do it myself. It's one of the really useful things I could remember ar arl Fella teaching me as a kid. He used to take bikes from the local *tip* and fix them up for all the kids on ar street. I remember I had this amazing *Raleigh Grifter* in blue. Lovely bike, like a *bmx,* but with chunky wheels. The only problem was I hated blue, bloody Toffee-men, so I painted it red instead. It ended up looking awful, with nasty brush strokes and dribbles of paint everywhere. To be fair ar arl Fella did warn us not to use gloss, but I didn't listen.

Thankfully though, I could remember how to change a tyre. By the time I'd finished, I felt closer to the *auld* man than ever. I remembered what he'd said about when you put your heart and soul into something. I realised it wasn't only true of allotments and bicycles. Somewhere, I must've had a huge part of that big daft Irish Fella's soul inside of me too. Just until now, I'd been too consumed with grief and alcohol to find it.

My only problem now was working out how this bloody *Facebook tingey* worked. But what else was my *brewstered* little brother for, if not sorting out technology. After all, he was utter shite at footy. So I clambered into the saddle of that *auld* bicycle and peddled it back to Ma's. Once I got there, I started pounding away at the door, but sadly there was no answer. I was just about to give up when Richie appeared at the window. 'I thought I told you we were isolating, Wayne,' he said, poking his head out onto the street.

'I just need some help with this phone,' I replied.

'Okay, but I'm not setting you up an account at Ladbrokes, if that's what you're after.'

'There's nothing to bet on my arl *meff*, the racing's cancelled,' I replied. 'I need to get on *Facebook*.'

'Okay, I'm coming down, but it's the last time. From now on it's through the window only.'

So my arl whacker Richie set me up on *Facebook* and I was at the races, so to speak. At first I found a lady who wanted a cabbage, which was easy to solve, seeing as I had a stack of those left over. I managed to get rid of most of the beetroot, but I struggled with the sprouts. It's no surprise really, as ar arl Fella used to say, the only difference between sprouts and bogeys is that children will happily eat bogeys.

Pretty soon, people wanted things I couldn't find on my arl Fella's allotment. So I dipped into my benefits and got them from the supermarket. I've got to be honest, it was all a little bit crazy. Maybe that's why the streets had been empty earlier, they must've all been here stripping the shelves bare, like a plague of locusts. Still, I managed to get a few bits and hand them onto people who really needed them. Most of them weren't able to come out and thank me themselves, but they did leave kind notes. As I replied to more people's messages, I asked them to leave the money on their porches, making a guess at what they thought their items were worth. Only so I could keep it going. I made sure everybody understood, if they couldn't pay, then it didn't really matter.

Funny enough, most people left too much money. Which I used to re-invest in more non-perishables for the food bank. Whilst I was absolutely knackered by the end of that first day, I had to say people had given me far more than I had given them. And I don't just mean the money. Sure my body hurt in places I never knew existed, but I had the best night sleep I'd had in years and I woke up the next day ready to do it all over again.

On my way over to the allotment to pick-up some more vegetables, I decided to swing past Ma's. It was dead early, but I knew she'd be up. I parked my bicycle up against the wall and tapped on the window of the front room. There she was, stood in her dressing gown with her rollers in. 'Bloody hell, Wayne,' she said. 'You gave me the fright of my life.'

'Sorry, Ma. I just came over to see if you needed anything.'

'What since yesterday?' She laughed. 'You big daft bugger, where are you really off to.'

'The arl Fella's allotment.' I said.

'What again?' she asked.

'Yep again,' I said, getting back onto my bike and riding off up the hill. 'Oh and I might have also popped over to say I love you.'

I knew she wouldn't say it back. She wasn't the sort of woman who found that word easy to say, not since ar Kenny. But as I cycled away, I did hear the window creak open a bit wider and her shout, 'I'm proud of you, son.'

And I thought to myself, *that'll do.*

As I cycled over to the allotment, I began to wonder how many years had passed since Ma had last said she was proud of me. I was already at the rickety old gate with the scarf tied around it when I realised. It was the final year of primary school. My teacher at the time was so fed up with my bad handwriting, he banned me from football practice. I remember my Ma going in and telling him what for. She accepted my handwriting could improve, but she was furious he hadn't bothered to read my story. I can't remember what that story was about, but I remember she really loved it. That was the thing about Ma, maybe she did find it hard to express her feelings, but if anyone from outside the family merely slighted us, she was onto them like a shot. I wondered if that was part of the reason we'd become a bit distant. She'd spent the last thirty years trying to get justice for Kenny, whilst I'd spent them completely and utterly *bladdered*.

By the time I'd loaded my basket with supplies, I realised there wouldn't be much point coming back tomorrow. Second day into lockdown and I'd already exhausted all of my arl Fella's hard work. Still, deep down I knew, I'd have to find an excuse, because with the *ozzy* closed, this was the closest I could get to him. It was then I noticed a few stones had appeared in the topsoil. I started to rake them and before I knew it I found my connection to the *auld* man once more. He was a bit of a mystery really. He showed his feelings a lot more readily than Ma, but he still didn't wear his heart on his sleeve. He wasn't how you'd imagine a Minister. For a start he smoked like a chimney. Still, I would probably describe him as a man blinded by his faith. That's not to say he ever pushed it onto others. He made us all aware that the only way to salvation was through the belief in Jesus Christ and pretty much left it at that. Occasionally, he'd make these somewhat arrogant remarks if you tried to help him with something, like repairing his *auld* Austin Allegro. He'd say, "Here I am doing the Lord's work and you think you can give me a hand." Although I found it more naive than anything. Let's face it, even God couldn't save that *auld* Allegro.

If you'd ever met him in the street, you'd never have guessed he was a Preacher. His method of trying to save you was much like how he taught me to change the bicycle tyre. He simply laid the little rubber patch and the glue onto the gravel, fetched a bucket of water, passed me the pump and said, "You'll work it out." It's not until that moment I realised, when you figure something out for yourself, the lesson stays with you a lot longer. In that way, it's far more powerful.

I'd just about finished raking up those stones by then, when I saw another one come flying over my head and land in the dirt by my feet. I turned around, completely mystified. There was nobody there, but it was the first time I'd felt

Kenny's presence since I'd laid off the drinking. 'Kenny you stupid *blert*, what did you do that for?' I asked.

'Just keeping you busy, my arl *meff*?' he replied.

'Busy?' I said. 'I've got enough to do. I'm off on my deliveries in a minute, if you want to tag along.'

'Sorry, pal. You go ahead.' Kenny said. 'But I'll see you soon.'

'Sure thing,' I replied. I must admit, it sent a shiver up my spine as I wheeled my bicycle back up the muddy lane and cycled away. Funny enough, that was the last I heard from ar Kenny for the rest of lockdown. But he did leave me a fresh smattering of stones on the allotment every day. Which I was most grateful for because it gave me an excuse to keep on visiting.

My first delivery that morning was to an elderly lady named Sandy. She hadn't posted what she wanted, a neighbour had done it for her. It was all very mysterious, but apparently, there'd be a note pinned to her door. When I eventually found her address, I noticed a little green card by the doorstep. At first I thought it must be her shopping list, but it was completely blank, so I had no choice but to ring the doorbell. When she finally answered, I was greeted by a white-haired *Judy*, with a ruddy complexion and something which resembled a smile, but might have been a grimace. She struggled to walk you see, but she was dead friendly. 'Hello, my dear,' she said. 'You must be the guy who delivers the shopping. Come on in.'

'I'm not sure if that's a good idea,' I said, thinking about my arl Fella. 'This virus is no joke you know.'

'That's why I've got the green card up,' she replied. 'I haven't got it.'

'I know that,' I said, trying to understand how she must've felt, but I knew if I went traipsing in and out of people's houses, I might end up doing more harm than good. By now I'd got myself a mask and gloves from the supermarket, so reluctantly I entered. Above her fireplace was a red and white scarf and pictures of her family. 'Oh, you're a Liverpool fan then?'

'Nope, a Gunner,' she replied, shaking her head. 'I suppose somebody's got to be.'

'I guess things haven't been the same since Wenger left.' I said, trying to empathise, after all, we'd been through some barren years ourselves until Klopp took over at Anfield.

'You can say that again,' she replied, handing me a little handwritten list.

Most of the stuff on it was organic and I knew it would be hard to get, but I promised to do my best. 'I'll bring it back in about an hour,' I said.

'Oh, it's not for me. It's for Graham opposite. He hasn't got anyone and he can't use a computer.'

'No problem,' I said. 'But are you sure you don't need anything?'

'I could do with some fresh veg,' she replied.

'Well, you're in luck,' I said, going back outside to my bicycle. First drop of the day and I'd managed to offload the last of my arl Fella's supplies. He'd have been absolutely made up.

I'm not going to lie, I couldn't get half of the stuff on Graham's list. Still, he didn't seem to mind when I returned. Now, if she was an Arsenal fan, then I had no idea what he was. Something entirely different, I guess. He was *auld* and wizened-looking, peering over his spectacles like the hunchback of Knotty-Ash. Apparently his sister had died of multiple sclerosis and it ran in the family. Seeing as he could hardly walk too, we agreed I could leave his shopping in a lean-to larder at the back, which had probably been the coal shed originally. He said he wasn't really into football, but we did get talking about *auld* black and white movies, most of which I'd never heard of, except A *Rebel without a Cause*. It was one of my arl Fella's favourites, I think that's how he used to picture himself, or Jesus. I couldn't quite remember which.

Whilst most of my drops were just one-offs, Graham and Sandy became regulars. I made sure I kept them well-stocked, as safely as I could. I persuaded Sandy to stop inviting me in, but she still kept that green card outside. Only now, it meant she was feeling ok. In fact, she told the rest of the street to do the same like a traffic light system, that way I could keep an eye on all of them.

Not everyone I helped was so kind, there was this one lady who didn't leave any money. I didn't mind, like I said, I was running at a surplus and I didn't want to leave anybody short. But when I had a nose around on her *Facebook* profile, I discovered all these nasty racist posts, blaming *bloody foreigners* for just about everything, including the coronavirus. But I let it go. Like my arl Fella would've said, "Help them all and let God sort it out."

By the time ar Kenny's Anniversary came along, I realised just how much I had changed. Other than the stone throwing incident at the allotment, I hadn't heard from Kenny in ages, but I felt stronger for it. Maybe cycling ten-miles a day had helped. Ar Richie had helped me download a *appy* thing, so I could keep track of it. I'd stopped drinking too and I hadn't even been to a single meeting. But that wasn't the only reason I felt better. In all those years I'd spent *bladdered*, I'd felt completely and utterly worthless. Only now, in helping others, had I managed to change that.

It ended up being the first year I didn't spend Kenny's anniversary in my flat, at the bottom of a bottle. Without his constant chatter in my ear, I'd finally been able to hear other voices in my head. Although I hadn't been able to visit my arl Fella, it was his voice I heard loudest of all. Not just on his allotment, or when I fixed the bicycle tyre. I heard him in each and every one of those people I'd helped. Graham, Sandy, even that crazy racist Judy. And it was him who told me to go and sit by the Mersey that night. It's where he first came to work when he arrived in Liverpool, all those years ago.

I don't know whether there was something special about being by the water, I knew it was often mentioned in the bible. But it's there, where I finally heard another voice. It's then I realised how that day a month ago would be remembered. Well, for me at least. *Sixteen, zero, three, twenty-twenty*, was the day I'd been reborn. Whilst I wasn't ready to follow my arl Fella and put on the *auld* dog-collar just yet. I'd found God. I'm not sure whether I would even tell Ma, let alone ar Richie or Lozzle, I was worried they might laff. But I knew what my arl Fella would say.

Amen.

Chapter 17
Richie Kennedy
16th March 2020

When the hotel manager came up and told me they were closing, it wasn't difficult to pack my things. After all, I hadn't brought much with me. A few shirts, a couple of pairs of trousers, I hadn't even bought any casual clothes for lounging around in. I knew my arl Fella was pretty ill when Ma had called and, whilst I hated to admit it, I got the feeling he wouldn't be here long and neither would I.

It was obvious now, I would have to go and stay at Ma's until this whole shit-storm passed over. She was desperate for me to sleep there in the first place, but I'd used the excuse that my car wouldn't be safe. Of course I knew it would. It had something called sentry mode, which filmed anyone who got within two metres. There was no point trying to steal it. The car would literally take your photo and upload it onto the internet.

Don't get me wrong, there was absolutely no bad blood between us, it's just we'd become a little distant over the years. Part of that was her fault, she'd obviously spent the past three decades fighting for justice for ar Kenny. With all the setbacks over the years, she'd become a little bit cold at times. Although I had to admit part of it was my fault too, after all, I'm the one who'd moved two-hundred and twenty miles away. I guess we all had our own way of dealing with things.

As I got into my car to drive over, for once I was annoyed about all the technology at my fingertips. The phone was ringing and, before I knew it, I'd picked up on hands-free. 'For God's sake Mags, now isn't a good time,' I said. 'Please can we just keep things between our solicitors?'

'Come on, Richie,' she replied. 'We were married for three years.'

'Eighteen months, Mags,' I said. 'But who's counting?'

'Was that all it was?' she replied.

Bloody expensive eighteen months if you asked me, I thought, but I didn't bother saying it. 'Ok, look I'm really busy this morning. What do you need?'

'Are you still in Liverpool?' Mags asked.

'Yep, I'm *gonna* be here for the foreseeable future now.'

'Great,' she replied. 'I was just wondering about the flat.'

My flat, I thought, but I didn't rise to the bait. 'It went onto the market yesterday.'

'But I doubt it's going to sell quickly now,' she added.

She had a point. It was a great flat. A perfect location on the South Bank and everything, but these were unusual times.

'Well, you won't be getting your divorce settlement until it does, if that's what you're thinking.'

'No, I wasn't Richie,' she said and suddenly I detected an air of vulnerability to her voice. 'I was wondering if I could move back in for a few weeks, just until I get myself sorted.'

'What about Simon?' I asked.

'Oh, he's at his Mum's because of this virus,' she replied, but I knew there was more to it than that.

'Ok, but only you. And just until it sells, Mags,' I said, not wanting to get into another argument.

'Thanks, Rich,' she said. 'Let me know if you want to come down and clear out any of your stuff.'

'I will do, Mags.' I said. 'But I've got to go now, I've got a lot on.'

When I arrived outside Ma's, I set up the sentry mode and went inside. I must admit, I was still proud of the old girl. The car that is. She'd pretty much saved my life during Saturday's punch-up. Despite the fact my cheeks still ached, I couldn't deny how fun it had been. Not only had I saved the day, like Michael Knight, but I'd also made amends with my brother Wayne. I wondered if it was the same for women, but as sexist as it might sound, sometimes men just needed a good old-fashioned punch-up to clear the air. Thankfully, this time it wasn't Wayne and I punching each other.

Despite arriving in a positive mood under the circumstances, I'd only been around Ma's for five minutes before I began feeling claustrophobic.

'Do you want a cup of tea, luv?'

'Do you want me to make your bed up, dear?'

'Have you got any laundry which needs doing?'

You get the idea. I knew she meant well, but no wonder Wayne and I had grown up with the characteristics of cavemen. 'I think I'll just pop out and get you some shopping, Ma,' I replied. 'I heard on the news the supermarkets are already struggling to cope.'

To be honest it was pretty bad when I arrived, although there had been a delivery in the night and the staff were working double time to get it out on the shelves. Thankfully, with a few swaps here and there, I did manage to get almost everything we needed. As I returned, who should be swinging by but ar Wayne. Bless him, he'd bought Ma round some veg, although God only knows where he'd got it because it looked pretty manky, covered in dirt and grubs. I couldn't invite him in, even though I wanted to, but he gave Ma this lovely *auld* radio which I realised had sentimental value. In exchange, I managed to give him my *auld* mobile, just to stay in touch, should something happen to ar arl Fella.

That's when my lockdown really began. After the previous day's chaos with the football being cancelled, suddenly it was like my phone had been cut off. I guess I'd been so busy with work of late, I'd forgotten how uncomfortable silence could be. So I went on the hunt for some batteries for my arl Fella's radio. 'Have you got any idea where they might be, Ma?' I asked.

'Kitchen draws are your best bet, luv,' she replied.

'I wished you'd have told me you needed some, I would've got some from the shop,' I said.

'Well, I didn't know Wayne was going to bring the radio, did I?' she snapped.

This was going to be a long few weeks. I must've spent ten minutes, rummaging through cutlery, carrier bags, old phone chargers, until I finally found a half-empty packet of C-sized batteries. They were in the bottom draw, which Ma called the *odds and sods* draw. It's funny, but I had a similar draw at my place, despite the fact I'd kept my apartment dead minimalistic. Mags constantly disapproved, claiming it looked too clinical to be a home. It made me smile, maybe Ma and I weren't that dissimilar after all. 'I found them, Ma,' I said. '*Gissus* the radio.'

She came in and placed it carefully onto the draining board. It obviously meant a lot to her, although I wasn't sure why. It took a while to get the *auld* batteries out. They'd leaked acid everywhere and I had to clean up the terminals with *WD-40*, which again I found in the *odds and sods* draw. To be honest, I was useless at fixing things. It's not that ar arl Fella hadn't tried to teach me, but he had this method of getting me to figure it out for myself, which was totally lost on me. In the end, my DIY skills could be explained by a very simple flow chart. Was it supposed to stay still? Then use *duct tape*. Was it supposed to move? Then use *WD-40*.

Anyway, after getting my shirt sleeves really filthy, I finally got this radio working. Even though I usually hated *antwacky* stuff like that, even I had to admit it was a lovely *auld* thing. Powder blue and covered in chrome grills like an old classic sports car. We eventually got it tuned into some old rhythm and blues station and Ma patiently waited for them to play a bit of Van Morrison, or *Van the Man,* as she called him. I knew it was the music she listened to when she'd fallen in love with my arl Fella, so I wasn't going to complain. But the sound quality of that *auld* thing was atrocious. If we were going to spend the next few weeks together, something was going to have to give, either my ear drums or my arl Fella's beloved transistor radio. So the first thing I did was order an *Alexa* on my phone. At first Ma hated it. 'It's like having a bloody ghost in the house,' she said.

But one night, I caught her downstairs whilst I was making a cup of tea and she asked it to play *Brown-Eyed Girl*. I snuck back to my room without her noticing, partly because I'd forgotten to put my clothes on. But I realised then she secretly loved it. The *Alexa* I mean, not me walking about the house naked.

My next purchase was a computer. Having been a secretary at a printers, Ma took to that pretty easily, but she did keep using it to research the Hillsborough case. In the end, I picked her up on it, but I wondered if it was a mistake. 'You've got to let it go Ma,' I said.

'I know,' she replied, much to my surprise. 'I wish I could be more like your arl Fella and turn the other cheek, but I can't.'

'We're not all made from steel like him,' I replied and we both cried.

It's funny, but that was the most open conversation we'd had in the past thirty years. Much to Ma's credit, she did start using that computer for other stuff. We found an online quiz for local people. For a bit of fun, it was Liverpool versus Everton fans. The whole thing was very cleverly designed, so you couldn't cheat using the internet and it was all done via

Zoom. Rather than facts, each round was a *guess the connection* question.

'What connects Alan Hansen with Harry Potter?' the quiz master asked.

'Scar on the forehead,' Ma replied, and quickly typed it in. It seemed she knew more about footy than me.

Although she let herself down with question two. 'What have chocolate éclairs and Everton got in common?'

Now, I knew the answer was toffee, but before I could get a word in edgeways, Ma had shouted at the top of her voice, 'They're both full of shit.'

I prayed the microphone was turned off so nobody could hear us. It was worse than watching *gogglebox*, which had become my guilty pleasure over the past few weeks. It was a TV show about real people watching TV. I know it sounds terrible, but it was hilarious. Apparently, some of the people were famous, but I hadn't got a clue who they were. Ma did though, it seemed in that way she was more up to date than I was too.

We also watched this documentary about a homosexual, polygamous man, who kept tigers on his ranch in America. Well, if you thought *gogglebox* was weird, then best swerve that one. Of course we watched a lot of news. You couldn't escape that. The figures of people dying were horrendous.

Knowing my arl Fella might become one of them, only made it worse, especially as we couldn't go and see him. Ma got daily updates from the *ozzy* and we both feared the worst every time the phone rang. But all she kept saying was, 'No news is good news.'

In that way, it was a bit like the war effort. The worst thing I heard on the *telly* was this bloody government advisor. It seemed, whilst I wasn't even allowed to go in and hold my arl Fella's hand, in what might be his dying hour, this *meff* had gone to Barnard Castle to get his eyes checked. Bloody typical, one rule for them and another rule for us. For that reason, I tried to stop Ma watching the news and I would always get a game out when it came on. We played a lot of *Uno* and *Monopoly*, but our favourite was *Scrabble*. We made up different themes, so you could only lay words on a certain topic. It was all going well until we did a Liverpool Football Club round. We allowed proper nouns, such as players' names, but Ma just wouldn't have it when I said there were two *A*'s in Grobbelaar. Boy did we have a row. 'You're a bloody cheat, Richie. You always have been a right Maradonna,' she said. 'With your fancy job. You think you're so much better than us lot.'

I think she meant prima donna, but I didn't want to correct her. We were just getting under each other's feet, that's all.

Other than Wayne's occasional visits, it was just the two of us. We even got the groceries delivered after that first week. Whilst I had been dreading it at first, it turned out to be just what I needed. I knew first-hand how serious coronavirus was with my arl Fella in the *ozzy*, but even he would've said, "It's an ill wind that doesn't blow some good." Those ten weeks allowed me to do something which I hadn't been able to do for thirty years. They allowed me time to reconnect with my arl *Gerl*. God bless her.

I would've stayed longer too, but on the twenty-eighth of May, I couldn't help but catch the news. There'd been a murder in America, a black man by the name of George Floyd. It seems he'd pretty much been lynched by the Police. Suddenly, my phone lit up. Working in football, I was already aware of *Black Lives Matter* and the FA's *Kick It Out* campaign, but suddenly many of my clients were calling me, asking if they could make statements. Of course I told them to go ahead, 'If you lose any sponsorship for making a stand on this one, then they aren't sponsors we want to be associated with anyway,' I said, to anyone who asked.

It was a mad few days. In between calls from clients, the estate agents rang and said there had been an offer on the flat. All of a sudden, I had to go to London to clear it up and deal with the dreaded Mags situation. I also had to call Amber, I wondered how she was coping with all of this. 'Hello, stranger, sorry I haven't been in touch,' I said, realising we hadn't spoken since lockdown began.

'It's okay,' she replied. 'I guess it's been a mad few weeks.'

'You can say that again,' I added. 'Have you seen the news?'

'Seen it!' she said, suddenly sounding angry. 'I've been living it for the past thirty years.'

'I suppose you have,' I replied. 'Which is why I'm calling.'

'Ok,' Amber said. 'What have you got in mind?'

'I'm going to London to clear out my flat tomorrow, there's going to be a rally. Do you want to come? I just feel I need to show my support. Especially as a white guy who represents many people of colour.'

'You can say black,' Amber said. 'To be honest, people of colour is a whole different thing anyway.'

'Oh, my mistake,' I said, somewhat embarrassed.

'Don't worry about it,' she said.

'So will you come?' I asked.

'I'm already packed,' she replied. 'But I'd love a lift down. I didn't fancy risking public transport.'

'It would be my pleasure,' I said.

I pulled up outside hers about nine, having given the car a super charge at Stanley Docks. The whole process only took about forty-five minutes, which was a relief because there was a memorial to the Titanic down at Stanley and it got me thinking about my arl Fella. Apparently, his grandfather helped build that boat or something.

Amber got in, looking as heavenly as ever. She'd obviously been taking good care of herself despite the lack of training during lockdown. 'Good to see you've kept in shape,' I said. 'I wasn't lying about this trial. Liverpool Ladies are going to be in touch the moment the season starts back up.'

'To be honest, it's been dead easy with Maccy's being shut. But if they don't use, *Return of the Mac,* as the theme tune when it reopens, then this whole lockdown will have been for nothing.'

'I haven't been deliberately ignoring you,' I said, as we both chuckled. 'I've just been a bit busy with Ma.'

'I know,' she replied. 'How's your arl Fella doing anyway?'

'Still no change, somehow that virus can't seem to take him. But I'm not getting my hopes up.' I said, desperate to change the subject. 'I've missed you, anyway.'

'Me too,' she said, patting the dashboard, obviously referring to my car.

'Oh, that's charming.' I replied.

'I might've missed you as well, Richie,' she giggled. She had a beautiful laugh, it was as if she was the only person in the room and she didn't care what anyone else thought.

We made good time down to London, seeing as the roads were more or less empty. Thankfully, the Tesla could not only do the entire journey on a single charge, it could also do it in under four hours. We listened to a lot of music on the way down. At first I chose the tracks. I hate to admit it, but during lockdown, I'd got really into my Ma's Van Morrison songs. Amber kept saying they were dead *antwacky* and ribbing us for it. In the end, I let her choose and she went for Sam Cooke's, *A Change Is Gonna Come*. We both sang along and I'd like to think we were in perfect harmony.

I knew it was something of an anthem for the *Black Panther* Movement, back in the day. But it felt really fresh all the same, just as important now as it ever had. It wasn't until we got to the verse about him being on his knees and his brother knocking him, that I became a bit tearful, though. It got me thinking of the years I'd ignored ar Wayne, as well as the time I'd spent trying to shut out ar Kenny. But when Spotify followed it up with Marvin Gaye's *What's Going On*, everything came pouring out. My arl Fella, Kenny, Ma. I was in absolute bits. 'What's wrong?' Amber said, noticing me crying.

I put the car into self-drive and looked at her, really looked at her. 'Just thinking about Kenny,' I said. 'I suppose I should be over it by now.'

'Tell me about it,' she said, obviously referring to her mother. 'The years just keep flying by, but I still think about her.'

'Thirty-one years and six weeks,' I said, unable to hold her stare.

She reached across and stroked my leg. It was funny, but it reminded me of a story I'd told ar Wayne on my way up from London. Only that was fake and this was real. In all honesty, there hadn't been anybody since Mag's, least of all my intern. It was just a bit of banter to try and impress my big brother on a boring road trip. I'm pretty sure *gerls* didn't really fall at your feet just because you drove a nice car. Or if they did, it definitely didn't stretch to guys like me. 'The fifteenth of April, nineteen eighty-nine,' I said. 'Hillsborough.'

Amber suddenly looked shocked. 'You never told me Kenny died at Hillsborough,'

'I'm sure I did,' I said.

'I think I would've remembered that,' she replied. 'You need to realise, you don't open up that much, Richie. Like when you invited me to see your Ma. I wasn't really prepared for all that *under-the-microscope-shit* from your sister.'

'You sound like my *soon-to-be ex-wife* now,' I said, drying my eyes. 'I'm sorry I put you through it. We'll wait until you're ready until we tell Ma if you like?'

'Thanks,' she said. Then she cranked up the volume on the stereo. Spotify had seamlessly faded into Traccy Chapman's *Fast Car.* It was still a bit of a tear-jerker, so I stuck the Tesla back into manual-drive and left my emotions on the tarmac. Amber continued to sing out loud and that's when I realised. She had a much better voice than me.

When we first arrived, it was all pretty calm. Most people were in masks and everyone I saw was respecting social-distancing. I had worried I'd be the only white guy there, but I needn't have bothered. There was such a mixture of races. It really lifted my mood to see people coming together. Despite everything that was going on, they obviously thought it was important to make a stand.

By the time we got to Hyde Park Corner, things became more hectic. There were far too many people in one place, crammed together like sardines. With the crowds making it impossible to move, we stopped for a while and listened to the numerous people making speeches. Some were celebrities, others were just ordinary folk from their own communities, who felt they needed to speak out. As a black preacher took up the microphone and gave an impassioned sermon, I got thinking of my arl Fella. He'd have definitely come along if he could. Despite all the work which still needed to be done, there was a real sense of hope in the air.

We marched on, but it was all getting a bit fiery now. Skirmishes were breaking out between the police and the protesters. Somebody had let off a flare and it had startled one of the Police horses. It was hard to tell who was to blame. There were just too many people in one place. It was the reason I'd stopped going to matches and begun dealing with my clients in offices and boardrooms. It reminded me of Hillsborough. I turned to Amber and I'm not sure if I handled it correctly, but I just said to her, 'I've got to go.' Then I turned back and headed for the safety of my old apartment on the South Bank.

Chapter 18
Lauren Kennedy
16th March 2020

Things were a bit crazy going back to work. It wasn't that busy at first, but still it was a struggle. I'd been off for the best part of two weeks because of my arl Fella's stroke and I hadn't been up before nine for a while. To make matters worse, I'd been forced to move out of Ma's because of the risk of passing on the infection. Richie was going to keep *douse* over her in my absence, but I'd been unceremoniously dumped into the *Travelodge*.

I didn't mind for the first week. The bed was pretty comfy and, despite the drab colours, there were plenty of bacon sandwiches to go around. Work was pretty easy too. Most of the more routine cases were cancelled. Accident and Emergency had never been so quiet, which had a knock on effect to ICU. It seemed all those people who used to come in with an ingrowing toe-nail had got the message to stay away.

We spent most of our time cleaning and having morning briefings. They were always chaired by Yannis. He was everybody's favourite doctor. He was this crazy Greek guy with a mass of black curly hair. He used to swear every other word, but only in his native language, so the patients didn't understand. No matter what happened on shift, he was never actually flustered. It was more like a pantomime than real swearing, and most of us threw in the odd *malakas* here and there. To be honest, the real reason we all loved Yannis was because he was always the calmest head on shift. In many ways, he reminded me of Bruce Grobbelaar, with his porno moustache and his crazy mannerisms, but just like my arl Ma's favourite keeper, he was a safe pair of hands.

That's why I'll never forget that briefing, at the beginning of the second week. By then even Yannis was showing the strain. 'Can I have all your attention, please,' Yannis said. 'You've all been doing a great job changing your protective aprons and visors in between patients, but I'm afraid I'm going to have to ask you to stop.'

'Isn't that dangerous?' one nurse asked.

'It's not ideal,' Yannis replied. 'And if your patient has tested positive for coronavirus, you should still change. But if they have not, you're going to have to make the one you're wearing last a bit longer. There's a national shortage.'

By then I knew it was serious. Not only because of what he was asking us to do, but because he hadn't sworn once. That was the week it really started to kick-off. One morning we had over a hundred cases come in all at once. Some of them were made to wait outside in ambulances, until we figured out what to do with them. The following morning

Yannis held another briefing, only now he looked exhausted. Apparently he'd been on shift for over thirty hours. 'Sorry, guys, I've got some more bad news,' he said. 'We're running low on tests, so if anyone has symptoms I'm going to need you to self-isolate for fourteen days.'

'That's not possible,' I said. 'We'll have nobody left on shift by the end of the week.'

'I know,' Yannis replied. 'But it's the best we can do right now. We'll try and prioritise you for a test if this happens. But if you can't get one, others will just have to pick up the slack. There's a sheet to sign up for overtime going up on the notice board later.'

I was proper tired after that day. To make matters worse, the *Travelodge* had closed the kitchens, so I had to stagger all the way across town to the supermarket. Having spent twelve hours on my feet, rushing between patients, it was that or nothing to eat for my tea. Imagine my horror when I discovered the shelves had been stripped bare. 'You should've been here when they arrived,' the *Judy* on the till said, looking almost as tired as I did. 'People were so rude to us. I'll see if I can get you a few bits from the stock-room.'

That's when I realised, it wasn't only us suffering. When I got home I was close to putting something on my Instagram about it, until Giles called me up on *Zoom*. 'Hey, babes. How are you holding up?' he said. 'You must be shattered.'

'Shattered and hungry,' I said, although truthfully the *gerl* in the shop had found me a pot-noodle to keep me going.

'Well, I've got a surprise for you,' Giles said. 'But I need you to take your phone and go up onto the roof to collect it.'

'Giles!' I said, sounding a little more frustrated than I intended. 'I'm too tired for this.'

'Come on,' he said. 'I promise it'll be worth it.'

I staggered up the stairs and out of the fire-escape, stepping out into what looked like the top-floor of a multi-story carpark, only there were no cars. 'Are you ready?' Giles asked.

'Ready for what?' I snapped. But then I heard a faint humming and spotted something approaching from the distance. 'That better not be you in your *arl* Fella's helicopter.'

'Even I don't have that level of clearance,' he said. 'But keep your phone on and stay put.'

Now ar Richie is the nerdy one out of the three of us, but even I guessed that drone must've been using the GPS on my phone to track me. It slowly hovered down and dropped a huge basket full of food. There was fresh fruit, vegetables, bread and soup. Along with a few *smellies* and some lush bubble-bath. 'Oh, Giles. What did I do to deserve this?'

'You're saving the bloody country, that's what,' he replied.

I felt awful for snapping at him, but I properly made it up to him later. I'm not going to tell you exactly how, but let's just say it involved my phone, a late night *Zoom* call and a whole lot of bubble bath and we'll leave it at that.

The next day was another mad one at work. It was so hectic, it reminded me of the final episode of Game of Thrones when that mad *Judy* flew over the city on her dragon and set fire to it. It was utter carnage. So many patients were coming through, I couldn't even remember their names. Although one lady stuck out in my mind. Her name was Peggy. She was a spritely little thing, despite being over eighty and having a hacking cough. 'I like you,' she said, as I checked her vitals. 'You remind me of my granddaughter.'

'That's nice,' I said, trying to raise a smile. 'Do you see much of her?'

'Not much,' she replied. 'She moved to Australia a couple of years ago with her job.'

'Oh, that's sad,' I said.

'You're telling me,' Peggy replied, a little short of breath. 'But it's ok. I grew up in the war, so I'm pretty tough.'

199

'I bet that puts this coronavirus into perspective,' I said, trying to remain positive.

'Not really,' she replied, much to my surprise. 'Ok, so we had the bombs and that. But we also had each other. With this coronavirus, I haven't seen another soul in weeks.'

'Well, maybe that's for the best,' I said, trying to keep her calm. 'We don't want you catching it.'

However, by the look of her temperature and that nasty cough she was trying to supress, I got the feeling it was already too late. So I marked her down as urgent and sent her off to Yannis. There was a long queue of patients by now, but I had to nip off to change my apron, even though she hadn't tested positive. She had too many symptoms to ignore. As I was getting changed, I suddenly felt dog-tired. It was no surprise, it had been one hell of a morning. But this was different. I already had the beginnings of a sore throat and I'd lost my sense of taste. I told Yannis on my way back down the corridor, but he just took one big step back and said, 'You need to go home, immediately.'

'But Yannis, there's a tonne of patients waiting,' I protested.

'I don't care,' he said. 'There'll be even more if you go back on shift.'

So, as guilty as I felt for letting my colleagues down, I went straight to the *Travelodge* and locked myself in. Although I had to walk a mile and a half because I didn't want to risk spreading it on the bus. Funny enough, I didn't feel too bad by the time I got into bed. Maybe the fresh air had done me good, but I was happy all the same to hear from Giles, when he called me on *Zoom*. 'Hey, babes, I was just thinking about you?' I said, as I turned on my camera.

'Why are you about to have another bubble bath?' he asked, eagerly.

'I'm afraid not sweetie,' I said, blushing. 'I've been sent home from work.'

'What did you do now?' he asked.

'Nothing, I swear,' I couldn't help but *laff*, it seemed he already knew me too well. 'Don't get worried, but I've got a few symptoms?'

'Like what?'

'Nothing serious, just loss of taste and a sore throat,' I said, trying not to alarm him. 'Don't worry, you can't catch it from a virtual bubble bath.'

'Not funny, Lozzle,' he said, sounding really concerned. 'I'm worried about you.'

'Well, don't be.' I said. 'But you could do me a favour if you want.'

201

'Just name it,' he replied, confidently.

'You know how your arl *Fella* runs a couple of big firms?' I asked. 'Does he ever do background checks on people?'

'Well, he's not MI5 if that's what you mean, but there is a guy who handles that kind of stuff on behalf of the family.'

'Oh my god!' I screamed. 'Did you get me checked out?'

'Not, yet.' He *laffed*. 'Why, do I need to?'

'Oh, *shurrup*,' I said. 'Look, can you get him to take a look at this Amber Andrews. The one ar Richie's been parading round as ar niece.'

'I could get him to dig around a little,' Giles said. 'What do you want to know?'

'Well, duh,' I said. 'Her arl Fella's name on the birth certificate might help and her date of birth.'

'Ok, sweetie. Give me a couple of weeks and I'll get back to you,' he said, blowing me a kiss. 'Now, get some rest, you. I meant it when I said I was worried.'

Those next few days were when things really started to get rough. The sore throat got worse, along with the loss of taste and I had this terrible dry cough. But overall, it probably wasn't any more serious than the flu. The hardest thing was not being able to get updates on my arl Fella's progress. Obviously I wasn't allowed to treat him when I was on the ward. It was against patient-practitioner privilege. But my friend Karen had been keeping a special eye on him for us and keeping me in the loop if anything changed. It seemed so unfair that I could treat other people's dying relatives, but I couldn't do anything to save my own.

I felt much better by the second week, but I still wasn't allowed to return, despite the fact I was desperate to find out how Peggy was doing. On the thirteenth day, I finally got a text message, saying I had a test booked. Still, I had to traipse all the way across town to the local *Ikea* car park. It seemed they just assumed everybody who worked at the NHS had a bloody car. In the end I got soaking wet, standing in this long queue, between two battered Ford Mondeos as it pissed down with rain. Eventually, I got seen by a man in full protective gear, who swabbed my throat and nose before letting me go. Apparently, I tested negative. Although I didn't get the results back for another two weeks. By then I'd already gone back to work, seeing as I hadn't had any symptoms for fourteen days. I guess I'll never know if I had it for sure because I didn't get the antibody test. They just weren't available then.

On my first shift back I really wanted to give Yannis a big hug, who was looking really worse for wear by then. Obviously I wasn't allowed. The next thing on my list was to check on Peggy. It broke my heart when Yannis told me. She passed away, alone in a bed, whilst I'd been off sick.

I wasn't the only one struggling to cope. It was later that day Yannis had his melt-down. He completely lost it when he was interviewed by the local press, saying, 'It was disgusting what we'd had to put up with without the proper equipment.' Most of us, like me, would never know if we'd had this virus. But I'm pretty sure Yannis must have had it. He was the first on shift every morning and the last to go home every night, even if sometimes that was the following day. But if he did contract it, he covered his symptoms pretty well and he did it with the best intentions. He was like the captain of a sinking ship. If it was going down, then he was going with it.

That week was about the same time as the Black Lives Matters protests. Whilst that crazy Greek doctor, Yannis, was only a touch darker than me, he was still a foreigner. I couldn't get over why so many people were posting such racist right-wing bullshit online. Didn't they understand this magnificent bunch of doctors and nurses holding their beloved country together were basically a ragtag army of immigrants. Thankfully, it was sometime about then when they cancelled the applause too. A good thing if you asked me. Don't get me wrong, it was nice to be appreciated, but it was all starting to feel a bit contrived. After all, what we really needed was the right tools to do the job. Not a bloody clap and then sent straight back onto the battlefield with rusty old rifles which couldn't shoot straight.

Before I knew it, a few months had passed. Looking back, the whole experience had broken me beyond repair. I'd suffered plenty of loss working as a nurse for the past eight years, but it wasn't until Peggy died that I sobbed my heart out. Maybe it was because my arl Fella's condition was so similar. But somehow, that stubborn *auld* man hung in there. I wondered if it was ar Kenny watching over him because, despite everything, he was actually making progress. According to Karen, they were even considering moving him back on the stroke ward. He no longer tested positive for coronavirus, and he didn't have any symptoms. But he was still out-cold and his coma was no longer being medically induced. I just prayed he wasn't suffering.

But I think the one thing which really kept me going in my darkest times was ar Giles. His calls every night, the hampers of food and those bubble baths, brought us closer. Even though we were miles apart, with his family forcing him to take refuge on the Isle of Man. I'll never forget what happened when he called me on that last night, just before lockdown was lifted.

'Do you want the good news, the bad news or the really bad news,' he teased, when he rang me on *Zoom*.

'Giles,' I said, sounding more than a bit of a mardy-arse. 'Just come out with it.

'So, the bad news is there was no father on Amber's birth certificate,' he said. 'But the really bad news was her date of birth. The fourth of March nineteen-ninety.'

It was eleven months after Hillsborough, so I knew what it meant. 'So she can't be ar Kenny's daughter.'

'No,' Giles said. 'But I have good news.'

'What is it?' I asked, still trying to process the bad news.

'You need to go back up on the roof for that,' he said smiling.

When I finally got up those stairs, which were like climbing a bloody mountain by now, I saw another of his little drones arriving, but this one dropped a handwritten note at my feet.

I know it's bad timing, but what would you say if I asked you to marry me?

After all the terrible things I'd seen over the past twelve weeks, I knew what I'd say. I'd say grab everything that's good in this world with both hands and hold it close to your heart. Only I didn't tell him that. 'I'd say you'd have to bloody ask me properly, in person.'

'Okay,' he said, hiding any disappointment.

What I also realised was his Ma was right about that fly-boy. He was a bit quick on the trigger. Just not how she thought, that's all. So I treated him to another private viewing with my bubble bath.

Chapter 19
Richie Kennedy
6th June 2020

As I approached my apartment block, the strangest feeling filled my stomach. Whilst I loved that modern building, with its polished steel and black glass, it no longer felt like home. Maybe Mags was right, maybe it was too clinical. I took the elevator up to the eleventh floor and checked my pockets to see if I'd remembered the keys. With everything going on, my head was all over the place.

Eventually, I found them in my bag and stuck them into the lock. Maybe I should've knocked first, but Mags was standing there in the open-plan living room, half-naked, in a loosely-fitted robe. Just for a second, I remembered exactly why I'd fallen in love with her. 'Sorry,' I said. 'I didn't mean to barge my way in.'

'Don't worry about it, Richie,' she said. 'It's nothing you haven't seen before.'

Of course, she was right. But still, it felt awkward. 'How have you been?'

'Fine, I guess,' she said. But I knew it was one of those *fines* women use when they really didn't mean it.

'How's Simon?'

'He's run off with his secretary,' she said, suddenly letting the floodgates open.

'Oh,' I replied. 'I'm not quite sure what to say. But he was always a bit of a prick if you ask me.'

'A lot of a prick, Richie,' she said. 'I wish I'd never...'

'Don't, Mags,' I said, interrupting her. 'It's too late for that.'

'I know,' she said. 'But just for the record, it was never you.'

'What was never me?' I asked.

'Everything,' she said. 'It's me that can't have kids, not you. It's me who cheated and it's me who's getting everything they deserve.'

'It's not all your fault,' I said. 'Somebody pointed out to me earlier that I might have problems opening up.'

'Might have?' she laughed.

We both did.

'So what now?' I asked.

'Well, we could start again,' she said, although I could tell she didn't really mean it. 'The sale hasn't gone through yet, so we could still pull out. Or we could carry on and use the money to move to Surrey, like we always wanted.'

'Like *you* always wanted, Mags,' I said. 'I'm not sure what's going on now, but I'm thinking about moving back to Liverpool to support my Ma.'

'I think that would be good for you,' she said. 'So do you want to argue over who owns what? For old time's sake.'

'Just keep what you want, Mags,' I replied.

I must admit, I'd been dreading dividing up our life. Not the money. I'd come to terms with that. But I hated the idea of my life being split into two piles and arguing over whose coffee mug was whose, or which one of us owned the DVD player. Which, let's face it, was totally obsolete nowadays.

Thankfully, we skipped that phase in our break-up. Instead, I just boxed up the few bits Mags didn't want and we curled up on the sofa to watch a film, with her still wearing just her undies and a robe. I had wondered if there might be one last hurrah. There had been some good times, like last year's Champions League semi-final, where Liverpool came from a three-nil deficit to put four past the mighty Barcelona, at Anfield. If you think that was impressive, you should've seen the sex we had afterwards. Whilst I only managed to score once, Mags must've writhed on top of me for a full forty-five minutes. I think she probably managed more goals than Liverpool that night. Still, the final turned out to be a bit of an anti-climax. Okay, Liverpool won two-nil, but Mags and I had a terrible row about not being able to have kids and a few weeks later she'd run off with Simon.

That last night with Mag's was more like this year's semi-final, when Liverpool put up a good fight but lost to a well-organised Atletico Madrid. Instead of the fireworks from the year before, we just held each other one last time. When morning came and it was time to leave, I was even a bit sorry to say goodbye. But thankfully, we both knew it was over and we'd made our peace.

I woke up early that morning, with what felt like a long, depressing drive ahead of me. As I got out of the elevator, I was trying so hard not to look back over my shoulder, I barely heard my phone ring. It was Amber. She was desperate to talk. It seemed she'd stayed overnight at a friend's, which couldn't have been far away because she arrived in under five minutes and met me just as I was loading the last bits and bobs into the boot of the car. 'Sorry I didn't stay,' I said. 'I had a few things to sort out and I really don't like crowds.'

'Don't worry about it,' she said, looking a bit sheepish, as she handed me an envelope. 'Promise me you won't open it until you get home.'

'What is it?' I asked.

'Don't worry, you'll find out,' she said.

'So aren't you coming back with me?'

'Nah, I'm staying on a bit longer,' she said and gave me a proper hug.

Just at that moment, Mags appeared. 'You didn't hang around.'

'It's not what you think,' I said, pulling away from Amber. 'She's my niece.'

'Pull the other one, Rich,' Mags said.

'Isn't that right?' I said, turning back to Amber, but she'd already started to walk away.

After giving the car another charge, I started the long drive home. I decided to give the *Spotify* a rest, so I could be alone with my thoughts. Usually it was my favourite part of driving electric, the contemplative silence, but without Amber it felt too quiet. Besides, the letter sat beside me on the passenger seat was too mysterious. Too tempting. So the moment I got onto the motorway, I stuck the Tesla into self-drive and opened it up to have a look.

Dear Richie,

What I have to tell you is so hard, I've decided to write it down. I know you've got every right to be angry, but hopefully if I get my words down right, one day you might understand and even be able to forgive me. It was really hard growing up, not just as a woman footballer, without the support of her mother, but also as a black woman footballer. Things are slightly better today, but I really didn't have a lot of role models to look up to. I think that's why Heskey was always my favourite player, as a kid. Most of us girls follow the men's game closely, I wonder how many male players can say the same. It's also why it meant so much to me when you offered to take me down to the protests.

I know you got your wires crossed with the 'people of colour' thing, but you're one of the good ones, Richie. You actually get it. That's why I feel so awful about what I've done. You see, it's not like us black people are asking for a lot. We're not even asking for equality, most of us aren't that optimistic. Please understand that we are not saying that other lives don't matter, we are just saying that Black lives do. I wonder what the alternative is. Would some people be happier if we were merely asking for Black lives to be considered mildly relevant, or maybe they'd prefer it if we just said Black lives don't matter. That's why we needed to make a stand, despite this virus. The fact your arl Fella is in hospital with that awful disease and you still supported our protest means the world to me.

Like I said, I will be forever in your debt for many things, but one of them is definitely giving me a ride down to

London. I remember putting Sam Cooke on the radio and you and I singing along to, 'A Change Is Gonna come.' You have an awful voice by the way. But I wasn't to know that Spotify would follow it with Marvin Gaye's 'What's Going On.' I didn't know it would bring up all those memories about your arl Fella and your brother. Please believe me, I definitely didn't know until then that your Kenny died at Hillsborough. I remembered you making some joke, that your wife said you never really open up. Well, whilst I think she's a total idiot for letting you go, she might just have a point there. I think you believe you open up, but honestly Richie, you're a bit of a closed book. It's like when you invited me to your Ma's, (I absolutely love your family by the way) and you said that I could probably picture where Kenny grew up because you'd mentioned it so much before. Well, I couldn't because you hadn't mentioned it even once. There's no way I would've come if I knew what I know now. You have to understand, I never had a family like yours and, whilst I know you're all going through a lot right now with your arl Fella, you should consider yourself very lucky. I'd do anything for a family like that. When I said my Ma died in childbirth, I was lying. The truth is, she was that broken by the loss of her boyfriend, which I guess must've been your Kenny, she gave in to a life of drugs and prostitution. Looking just like her, old men used *to stop me in the street and ask how much. God knows if they knew her, but it was not only disrespectful to me, it was disrespectful to her memory. So I made this story up about her dying when I was born.*

Which brings me to what I need to say. Having been raised by my Nan and now finding myself over thirty, I'd do anything for my break in football. You've seen Merseyrail Ladies, they're a great team, but they're going nowhere and they keep playing me out of position. So the scouts keep passing me by. When you came along, I genuinely fancied you. Although I'm not going to lie, that fancy car of yours did most of the heavy lifting. When I found out you were an agent, I just let you believe what you wanted to, to keep you interested. To be honest, I am still not sure who my arl Fella is. All I do know, is he's not a tenth the man yours is. And it was not until you told me about Hillsborough, I realised for sure it wasn't your Kenny. The dates don't quite tally up.

For that reason, please understand, I didn't plan any of this and I hope you can forgive me. I'd also like to say I completely understand why you didn't join me on the march in the end. If I'd been to Hillsborough, I probably wouldn't have wanted to stand in that crowd either. Still, you showed your support by bringing me down, you showed me what sort of person you are. A far better one than me. I realise the

*scout coming to my next match is probably cancelled now
and I totally understand. I probably don't deserve my shot
after what I've done. But all I wanted you to know is that I'm
sorry.*

Yours,

Amber.

Ps Thanks for the Maccy's it was lush x

I couldn't believe what I was reading. *How could I have
been so stupid? How could she?* I pulled over, not to
recharge or for coffee. I just stopped to take it all in. I read
the letter again a second time. In the end, I realised Amber
was right about many things. I didn't open up. I had been
carrying this weight around with me for too long. It had cost
me my marriage and very nearly my family. There was no
way I was letting her back anywhere near my Ma, but I
forgave her. Life was too short to carry grudges and I
probably would've done the same in her position. After all,
she didn't know Kenny wasn't her father until she discovered
the exact date of his death. She'd just gone along with it, as
much out of hope as anything else. Just like I had.

No sooner did I get back on the road the phone rang. It
was the *Plaza*, they said I could have my room back if I
wanted. I thought about it. I had a lot to process. My

217

marriage was well and truly over, my flat had been sold and I was officially homeless. Ok, I could go back to Ma's if I wanted, but as good as it had been to reconnect, we did drive each other crazy. I also felt guilty. I'd come this close to turning her world upside down with Amber. I wasn't sure if I could look her in the eye. So I decided to take them up on their offer.

I spent the next few days in my underwear. It wasn't how my arl Fella would've dealt with things, but like a big *gerl's* blouse I ate my feelings. Ice cream, mostly. As the week drew on, my phone began to ring again. They were drawing up plans to restart the football season and I needed to check with my clients to see who was willing to take part. That's when I got the phone call from the scout. I didn't catch his name, he just kept asking if I'd heard the news. 'What news?' I asked. 'You'll have to be a bit more specific.'

'The women's football is back this week,' he said. 'Less likelihood of crowds gathering, you see.'

'Yep,' I said. 'How does that concern me?'

'Sorry, Vicky Jepson gave me your number,' he said. 'She wants me to take a look at the Merseyrail Ladies striker in their final game of the season on Wednesday. Apparently, you represent her?'

'Oh, yeah,' I said, having completely forgotten about that. 'She'll be playing. But I'm not sure if I can make it.'

'It would make things easier if you would,' he replied. 'We're desperate for a centre forward. If she fits the bill, we want to push the deal through sooner rather than later.'

'Ok,' I said. 'But they have this habit of playing her at number ten.'

'Oh,' the scout said. 'That's going to make things tricky.'

'I will see what I can do,' I replied.

I definitely couldn't face calling her, so I sent Amber a text.

The scout is still coming on Wednesday, please try and get your coach to play you up front.'

'Will do,' she replied. *'And sorry for everything x,'*

We had a hell of a summer during lockdown and that Wednesday was no exception. As I pulled up to Admiral Park, a little after seven, it was still well in the twenties. A slight crosswind was blowing across the pitch, but other than that, it was perfect conditions. I deliberately arrived a little late to avoid Amber and found my man on the touch-line. There were a few people gathered around to watch, but it was obvious which one was the scout, with his clipboard and lightweight Liverpool jacket. 'I don't think you'll be needing the anorak,' I said.

'You never know in Liverpool,' he replied. 'So I take it that's your *gerl* playing at number ten?' he said.

I looked out onto the pitch. He was right, Amber obviously hadn't had any luck persuading her coach. 'Yep,' I replied. 'Unfortunately, they need a point to stay up and the coach feels the team is harder to break down with her further back. It's a shame, it's a total waste of her talent.'

'I'll be the judge of that,' the scout said.

With the new water breaks in each half, the game turned out to be more tactical than ever. Merseyrail were playing very compactly and, with Amber positioned much deeper, they were able to keep the ball for long periods. However, most of the game was still being played in their own half and they were very vulnerable to the *off-the-ball* pressure from Manchester Stingers. Amber used the ball well, holding it up and making clever passes sideways. There was one moment when she shook off her marker and played a lovely ball over the top to her strike partner, but unfortunately, it came to nothing. When the half-time whistle blew, it was still goalless. I jogged across the pitch and listened to the team-talk, which was taking place on the touchline, due to social-distancing. I couldn't hear everything, but I got the gist of things. 'More of the same,' the coach was saying. 'Forty-five more minutes and we're safe.'

I really wanted to intervene, but I knew it wasn't my place. I also realised the coach was right. A draw was enough to stay up and, in his shoes, I'd have probably done the same. As the second half began, I went back and stood next to the scout. 'So, what do you think?' I said, hopefully.

'There's no doubt she's got talent,' he replied. 'She uses the ball well and I can see she's a great athlete. What's her diet like?'

Don't say McDonald's, I thought to myself. 'All good,' I replied. 'She's a proper professional on that front.'

'Well, I need to see more from her this half,' he replied. 'Like I said, we need a striker, not a hold-up player.'

'Understood,' I said.

The second half was much like the first, with Merseyrail stubbornly holding out for a goalless draw. But as the second drinks break approached, Manchester's game became more intense, more physical. They pressed higher and higher up the park. With twenty-five minutes left, after a prolonged period of attack, they earned a free-kick on the edge of the box. Amber had found herself on the wrong side of her opponent and ended up making a clumsy tackle. The resulting free-kick was probably twenty-five yards out, but the Stinger's midfielder caught it sweetly. The ball flew past the keeper's outstretched hand and clipped the post, before bouncing wide. It was a real let off and it was definitely Merseyrail who were the most relieved for the interval.

Once again the coach urged them to keep going. But just as they were going back onto the field, he pulled Amber to one side. 'If we go behind, then I want you to go straight up front and look for an equaliser,' he said. And just like that, there was hope.

They'd only been re-started a couple of minutes and the high press of Manchester had earned them a number of corners. Every time the ball came into the box, there was a last-ditch tackle or a goal line clearance. It seemed to be a battle of who wanted it more now. With five-minutes to go, the pressure finally took its toll. A fierce drive bounced awkwardly across the Merseyrail six-yard box and the centre-half turned it into her own net. It was a disaster. Even I felt sorry for her. She'd probably been the best player on the park until then. Still, with that goal came Amber's opportunity. The fourth official held up the board for five minutes of stoppage time and Amber went up-front to play beyond her strike partner. She was like a hungry lioness, sniffing out her prey.

Manchester did their best to keep the ball for the next few minutes. Six passes forward, followed by a long ball back to the keeper, only to repeat the process. 'Well, this is it,' the scout said to me. 'Here's your *gerl*'s final chance.'

Stingers' keeper made another long clearance. As the ball crossed the half-way line, I was sure the ref would blow for time. She lifted the whistle to her lips and checked her watch. There was obviously time for one last run of play. The centre-back, who'd scored the own goal, won the ball in her own half and just launched a diagonal ball the length and breadth of the field. Amber was being marked and her opponent rose to meet the ball with her head. I was disappointed Amber didn't bother to go up with her, but then I saw the genius in her plan. With her back to goal, she tracked the ball with her leading shoulder. It was too high for the defender and it continued to sail across Amber's body. With her balance shifting to her opposite leg, she spun round, perfectly tracking the flight of the ball. It's probably the single hardest skill in the game. Only one time in a hundred would a player make contact with the ball when trying to volley on the turn. Even if they did, only one in a million times would they connect sweetly. Well, this was one of those times. Amber's right foot made such a thud on the ball, she must have left her laces imprinted into the leather. The ball dipped and swerved its way right into the top corner. It was even better than the goal she'd scored in her last game.

She ran over to the corner flag and just stood there like a goddess. Her teammates followed and swamped her, burying her in a heap of bodies. I wondered if they'd ever get the game restarted, but once they did, the ref only allowed the kick-off before blowing for time.

'Well?' I said, turning to the scout.

'I'm not going to lie,' he said. 'Money is tight. But she is world-class.'

'I know,' I said. 'And whilst it's only right you make a sensible offer, take it from me, that *gerl* would sell her own grandmother to play for Liverpool.'

'Understood,' the scout said, holding out his hand. 'I'll get something in writing sent over to you. But I think we've got a deal.'

I met his grasp and shook his hand firmly. 'You bet we have.'

The celebrations were wild in the technical area. Amber's coach was getting the ice-bucket treatment. The centre-back, who'd made the initial error and made amends with the final assist, was getting the plaudits. Amber wasn't amongst them. She'd made her way over to the touch-line to talk to me.

'Well?' she said.

'Well, what?' I replied.

'Look, I'm sorry for everything,' she said. 'But I just want a chance.'

'Don't be,' I replied, flinging my arms around her. 'You did right by my Ma and you've done right by Merseyrail by keeping them up. But sadly, you've played your last game at Admiral Park. There's some paperwork to sort out, but you're signing for Liverpool next season.'

'Really?' she said.

'Really.' I replied. 'Although I want my ten-percent of the signing fee.'

'Have the lot,' she replied. 'And let me buy you a Maccy's to celebrate. I hear they're back open for drive-through.'

'Go on then,' I said. 'But go and see your teammates first.'

Once again, I was left waiting outside the ladies changing room. Only now I felt like a total misogynist, as I tried hard not to imagine the scenes of celebrations which must've been going on inside. Finally, Amber emerged looking as radiant as ever, wearing a Liverpool shirt and a pair of tight shorts.

'What?' she said, catching me staring.

'Red's your colour,' I said.

'Damn straight,' she said. 'But right now it's time for the return of the Mac.'

We went to the same one as before, on Park Road. Only we had to eat it in the car this time due to social-distancing. Eight cheeseburgers later, she finally looked up and said, 'Thanks.'

'Thanks for what?' I asked. 'It was your shout.'

'Thanks for everything,' she said. 'I wouldn't have made it without you.'

'You know they've given me my hotel room back at the *Plaza*,' I said, hopefully.

'Have they now?' she replied.

'We could call it our second date?' I said.

'What was this then?' she asked.

'Foreplay,' I replied, squirting ketchup all over her fries.

I have to admit I was a bit nervous. After all, she was a professional athlete in her prime and we all knew I couldn't catch a pig in a jigger. There hadn't been anyone since Mag's and that night at Anfield when we turned over Barcelona. So I wasn't exactly match-fit.

Anyway, I won't bore you with the details. All I would say is my performance was much like that night in Istanbul, when Liverpool came back from three-down to beat Milan. Only Stevie Gerrard had nothing on me.

When I finally woke the next morning, with Amber wearing nothing but her Liverpool shirt and her lean

226

muscular legs wrapped around me, I just started laughing.

'What is it?' she asked.

'Nothing,' I said, knowing she wouldn't understand. It's just I couldn't get that *auld* advert out of my head with Ian Rush in the eighties. Maybe I wasn't even good enough to play for Accrington Stanley, but I was going to need more than a glass of milk to get over this one.

Chapter 20

Susan Kennedy

25th June 2020

I can't deny, part of me was relieved when ar Richie had to go down to London. We had been getting under each other's feet a bit. But once he left, boy did I miss him. Not only had he become my rock, but we'd settled into a routine of quiz shows and board games. In fact, with ar Lozzle gone, this was the first time I'd ever been on my own. I suppose you could call it classic *empty nest syndrome*.

With too much time on my hands, I just started grieving all over again. Grieving for Kenny, not that I ever stopped. But worst of all, grieving for Ezzy. I knew he wasn't dead yet, but the news from the daily updates weren't good. I desperately wanted to see him. Even if he wasn't awake. I wanted to hold his hand. There were things I needed to say to him, things I never got the chance to say when he was here. I didn't know what I would do if I didn't get to say them at all. It didn't bear thinking about.

I knew Ezzy was probably going to die in that hospital, it had just been going on too long now to imagine he would just wake up and be alright. I was no stranger to grief. I could write a book on it. In the early days when someone you love dies, it's like being at the scene of a horrible accident. You're just standing there and, however it happened, you can't move on. You literally have to be pulled away by those around you. I wasn't there when ar Kenny passed away. I never asked Ezzy what actually happened. I couldn't bear to think about what he went through. I was too consumed by the Kenny-sized hole left in my life.

I kept his room like a shrine. Still to this day, it remains untouched, with the nineteen eighty-eight league winning team on the wall, managed by his name-sake Kenny Dalglish, in his red and grey coat. I had one just like it, which I used to wear on the touchline when I would watch ar Kenny play. In some ways those players have become part of my memory of Kenny. Especially Bruce Grobbelaar, the Liverpool keeper at the time. He was no looker, although the bad moustache was a bit more fashionable back then. We probably had Tom Selleck in *Magnum P.I.* to thank for that. I just liked Bruce, not only for everything he did on that fateful day, but for the flamboyant way he played the game. I suppose every parent feels like a goalkeeper sometimes. You don't want to stop your kids living their lives and scoring their goals, but you want to be there to save them if it all goes wrong.

Slowly, I moved on. Although those first few paces were only baby steps, made backwards, with my eyes firmly fixed on my boy. You don't want to leave them, filled with some irrational fear you might forget what they look like. It might take a month, or it might take a year, it's different for everyone, but eventually you turn around and start moving on. That's when you start walking the road of grief, as I called it. It's a foggy road, filled with days when you can't see your own hand in front of your face. But you keep walking. You have to. Time won't wait. Of course you keep turning back. Each anniversary missed, their birthdays, or moments when you wonder what they'd be doing with their life now. Each time you turn, you try to stand still. Try to accept that you'll never see them get married, or you'll never dance the funky chicken with them on their eighteenth birthday. In some ways, you come to terms with each of those milestones, but before you can get your feet planted firmly on the ground, time forces you on. Time forces you further down that road.

Deep down, I knew Ezzy had walked that road alongside me when it came to ar Kenny. Each and every step. Only I never reached out and took his hand to thank him. It's not like I hadn't tried, but it always came out as some bitter remark like, 'It's alright for you to say turn the other cheek,' or 'No, I will not bloody drop it.' It wasn't until Richie came home I realised how difficult I can be at times. That was the

231

best thing to come out of this bloody virus. Although the worst thing was it might be too late to set the record straight with ar Ezzy.

Fed up of waiting by the phone for bloody updates, I took myself out that morning. I hadn't been out of the house since March. Whilst I knew I had to be careful, those four walls were closing in on me. I wasn't exactly sure where I was heading at first. It was a bit like walking that road of grief. I was just moving forward. In the end, I headed over to ar Ezzy's church, where I was greeted at the door by Pastor McTominay. He was a young Fella and there must've been a bit of Celt in him because he had thick auburn hair with strands of ginger in his beard. I'd met him a couple of times before ar Ezzy fell ill. You know you're getting *auld* when Pastors look young enough to be your son. Still, I liked him. He reminded me of ar Ezzy all those years ago. He was full of strength and energy, yet to be weighed down by the burden of time. I remember thinking how pleased Ezzy would be that his congregation were in such a safe pair of hands. 'Hello, Susan,' he said, in that serene way men of faith talk. 'It's lovely to see you.'

'Thank you,' I replied. 'Sorry I haven't been in lately, but I've been shielding.'

'Don't worry,' he said, reassuringly. 'Anyone would forgive you for not gracing us with your presence, what with everything your family is going through right now.'

I knew he meant well, but it still felt like a stone in my garden. We both knew I hadn't really played my role as a Pastor's wife. I'd lost my faith in God long ago, when ar Kenny died. But the last thing I wanted to do was bring all that up now, so I changed the subject. 'How's the food bank going?'

'Excellent, thanks to your Wayne,' he said. 'Chip off the old block that one.'

'Wayne?' I asked. I knew he'd been down the allotment a few times and, thanks to the years of hard living, he had started to look more like Ezzy's brother than his son. But I hadn't realised he'd kept up his arl Fella's work throughout the whole of lockdown.

'I think it was Wayne,' the Pastor said, picking up on my surprise. 'I've never actually met your other son, Richie isn't it?'

'No, it was definitely Wayne,' I said, trying to ease my guilt. 'I told him to pay you a visit.'

'Visit?' he laughed. 'He's been in almost every day. Whilst there's been lots of kind donations and, it's by no

means a competition, nobody has donated more than Wayne.
Ezzy would be so proud. You both should be.'

'We are,' I said. That's when I got the idea to visit Ezzy's
allotment and take a look at all of Wayne's hard graft. When
I arrived, I couldn't believe it. The place was immaculate, all
raked and weeded. He'd even tidied out the shed. He must've
dug out all the vegetables because all that remained was this
giant rose bush, which was now taking over the entire plot. It
was covered in the most enormous red blooms, flowers the
size of my hands. I remember Ezzy telling me about it once.
He said it was called *Susie* and that's why he'd planted it. I
knew he was lying. He never bought anything from the
garden centre back then. Things were too tight. It was also
typical of that sweet-talking son of a shipbuilder to make
everything into a romantic gesture. Oh my god, I missed him
so much.

It was then I decided enough was enough. I knew
everyone was just doing their job at the *ozzy*. After all, ar
Lozzle was one of them. But I had to see him. Even if it was
just through the glass. There were things I had to say and
they couldn't wait a minute longer. So I took a cutting of that
rose and I started off down that long road. Only now I wasn't
moving forward. I was heading back to the scene. I was

going to say all the things I needed to say to my husband, before it was too late.

I arrived at the *ozzy* and they still wouldn't let me in. Of course I understood, but I was furious, particularly after that government advisor went on his little jolly. I knew Richie had tried to hide it from me, but I wasn't daft. So I went around the building to look for the window onto Ezzy's ward. Lozzle had called to say he'd been moved back downstairs. Staring at him from behind the glass, clutching at that rose, I just froze. I don't know how long I was there, but the words wouldn't come. In the end, I was about to go when a nurse appeared. She carefully opened the window and lent out to speak to us. 'Hello luv,' she said. 'Is he your husband?'

'For his sins, yes,' I said. 'Is there any chance I could just hold his hand?'

The nurse shook her head. 'Not today, but I'll have a word with the Matron and see about tomorrow.'

'Would you?' I asked.

'Sure, but I can't promise anything,' she replied. 'In the meantime, give me that rose and I'll pop it beside his bed. I shouldn't really, but I won't tell anyone if you don't.'

Just like that, I set back off on that road of grief. Only bless that nurse because she kept her word. The following morning I got the call from the Matron granting me a special visit. She had warned me I would have to wear a mask and that I couldn't bring anyone else with me. So I didn't take much, as I hopped on the bus. Just his *auld* radio. I thought I could play him some music, seeing as the words might not come straight away. I needn't have worried though. Just seeing him there after all this time was enough to start me off. 'Dear Ezzy,' I said, my voice wavering a little with emotion. 'I know I've been hard on you, it's just I've been walking this long road of grief and at times I forgot you were there beside me. Maybe you made it look easier than I did. But I know it wasn't. It's because you're stronger than I am. Stronger than all of us.' By now I was in floods of tears, but there was one more thing I needed to say. 'Ezzy, my darling. It wasn't your fault at Hillsborough. There were a lot of people to blame. A lot of people who could've done their jobs better. But not you. You were the best husband and the best father a *gerl* could wish for.'

Obviously, he didn't wake up like they do in the movies. But I know he heard me because I felt him squeeze my hand. In that moment, I felt free. I still knew I was probably going to lose him, but if I did, then I'd said what I'd needed to say. So I just stood there at the beginning of a new road of grief and waited until that sweet nurse who'd arranged my visit came along to pull me away.

Chapter 21
Wayne Kennedy
25th June 2020

It had been nearly a week since they restarted the *footy*. About bloody time too. We'd waited thirty years for this and I thought they were going to *chief* us out of it with some bloody technicality. Ar first match had been dead cagey. A nil-nil draw with the blue-noses. It felt strange not being able to go. Even the Willow was still shut. Which was probably a good thing. I didn't need an excuse to get back on the lush and I was still trying to avoid the Deli Mob, until the betting shops reopened. So in the end, I just watched it at home on the telly.

It turned out to be a real disappointment. Ar team looked like they were still in their pyjamas at times. The lack of crowd didn't help matters. It meant both teams ended up treating it like a training match. Although the result didn't do us any harm. It meant we only needed two more wins to become champions now. I just missed the banter, that's all. We didn't really hate Everton. To be honest their fans had been brilliant over Hillsborough. If anything, we felt sorry for them. God knows how long ago it was since they won anything.

Things got better a few days later, with a four-nil demolition of Crystal Palace. Alexander-Arnold and Salah both rediscovered their form in front of goal along with Mane and Fabinho. Now we only needed one more win, against none other than ar Championship rivals Man City and our thirty-year wait would be over. Although it did leave the prospect for a strange twist. If they failed to win their game in hand against Chelsea, we'd be champions before we got to the Etihad. Whilst I'd rather do it on the pitch, I couldn't help but think how funny it would be if they had to give us the guard of honour in their own backyard.

With so much at stake, I had considered watching Man City in their game against Chelsea. But in the end, I couldn't bring myself to do it. City bored the pants off me. I'm not being biased because I'm a *Kopite,* but I don't think anyone outside of Manchester wanted them to win. After all, they'd pretty much tried to buy the league title with all their expensive imports. Even if they had won a few things lately, they lacked ar history. Despite what Noel Gallagher might tell you, City were more like the Charlatans than Oasis.

So that night, I decided to do something else, something long overdue. It would've been nice for my family to be there, but with everything going on at home and away, it just wasn't possible. Besides, explaining it to them would've been a bit like telling them I'd started buying my clothes in Carnaby Street. So in the end, I was glad it was just me and Pastor McTominay.

We'd become great friends over the past few weeks, with all my trips to the food bank, but still I was nervous. 'Hold still,' he said, as he held the bread to my lips. 'Oh Lord Jesus Christ, only Son of the Father, in giving us your body and blood to eat and to drink, You lead us to remember and confess Your holy cross and passion, Your blessed death, Your rest in the tomb, Your resurrection from the dead, Your ascension into heaven, and the promise of Your coming again.'

I swallowed hard and washed it down with a sip of wine. It was the first drop which had passed my lips in months. I must admit, I had imagined there would be a feeling of electricity passing through me too. But there wasn't. Maybe that had all happened back in March. All I did know, is I tended to make bad jokes when I felt nervous. 'I never knew my arl Fella was a *Farder Bunloaf*,' I said.

Pastor McTominay just laughed as he led me over to the font. 'He isn't. He's a Lutheran. But it really doesn't matter,' he said. Then he made the mark of the cross on my forehead and that was it. I was confirmed.

I didn't have any more deliveries left that night, but I did pop round to see Graham and Sandy. I'd convinced them both to get one of those walkers with the seats on the front and they were both sat outside, along with the rest of the street. Somebody had brought a big telly outside to watch the football. Neither of them were Liverpool fans, but you wouldn't have guessed. They were cheering along with the rest of the neighbourhood as the final whistle blew. It seems I'd missed it, but Chelsea had beaten Man City and Liverpool were already champions. 'You must be delighted,' Sandy said.

It's true I was. Not just about the football either. Tears were streaming down my face. It had been a long road, not just for the reds to reclaim the title. For me too. For Kenny, for all of us. So I just stood there and sobbed my heart out.

It wasn't a long cycle ride back home, but I decided to nip through Hackins Hey. It wasn't much of a short cut, but I was running on pure emotion by then and my legs were killing me. I knew it was a mistake when I saw them block off the far end of the alley. Six of these *blert*s, clearly Deli Mob. You could just tell. But, I fancied my chances of getting away because I had a bicycle and they didn't.

It was too tight to turn around, so I just peddled right for them. At the last minute, I leaped off my arl Fella's bicycle and let it roll straight for them. Then I turned on my heels and ran in the opposite direction. That's when I realised six more *blert*s had joined them at the other end of the alley. That's when I knew I was fucked. Proper fucked. I'd love to say I took all six of them on, but I didn't. I tried to tell them about the betting slip back at my flat. But to be fair, I wouldn't have believed that story either.

They gave me a proper hiding. But I stayed on my feet and covered up. Punches rained in between my arms, but I just gritted my teeth, or what was left of them. I'd taken a worse hiding over the past thirty years. It's not until the other six caught up with me that I went down. Now, I was helpless on the floor as these twelve disciples of evil gave me the kicking of a lifetime. I curled up in a little ball and just thought about my arl Fella. He was the hardest man I knew, cut from the steel of Motherwell and forged in the docks of Belfast. When they finally left me, I was pissing out blood everywhere. But I staggered to my feet, picked up my bicycle and shouted as loud as I could, 'It'll be a pig's foot in the morning.'

From there on, I walked instead of cycled. I just couldn't keep my balance. When I finally made it home and let myself in, I did think about calling an ambulance. But despite the fact I was black and blue, somehow, I felt alright. Maybe my arl Fella had watched over us. Or maybe it was Jesus. I don't know.

I ran myself a bath and slowly submerged my body. I must have dozed off for a while because I was freezing when I woke, shivering and everything. I gingerly wiped myself dry with a towel and started looking for some pain killers. I still couldn't find them anywhere. But I did discover a tiny dribble of rum left in that bottle of *Captain Morgan's* I opened the night I called Richie. Just a swig. For medicinal purposes. I was never going back onto the drink, I knew that now. That's how I knew I was no longer an alcoholic. Because back in those days, I'd never have been able to stop at one mouthful.

I took to my bed and looked across at the betting slip still sat there. It had cost me three beatings now by my counting, but the debt was paid. I wondered what good I could do with that money, as I slowly drifted off to sleep.

Chapter 22
Wayne Kennedy
2nd July 2020

A week had passed since my run in with the Deli Mob and there hadn't been any repercussions. Perhaps they'd left me for dead. Or maybe they'd finally let it go. After all, it wasn't really twenty-grand I'd borrowed. It was more like two and an extortionate amount of interest. All I did know is I ached all over and I'd been finding it harder and harder to wake up in the morning. Today was no exception, but I was desperate to pop in on Ma before the big match in the evening. It was Liverpool versus City. Finally, we'd been crowned champions and now they were going to be forced to give us a guard of honour before the kick-off. I'd have loved to be there in person, but the game was not only in Manchester, it was behind closed doors.

Sadly, despite the announcement they were to re-open the pubs, the bloody bastards had decided to postpone it until Monday. They knew us *Kopite*s would be going mad in boozers like the Willow all across Merseyside. So, it was probably going to be a lonely night in for me.

Despite sleeping through my alarm twice, it was still pretty early when I got to Ma's. Ar Richie was back at the *Plaza* after his trip down to London, so when I saw the downstairs light on, I knew it must be her. 'Hi, Ma,' I said, tapping on the window as I parked my bicycle.

'Bloody hell, Wayne,' she said. 'What on God's Earth has happened to you?'

'Would you believe me if I told you I fell off my bike?' I asked, having completely forgotten that my face still looked pretty banged up.

'You haven't been on the booze again have you, luv?' she asked.

'No, Ma,' I said. 'That's something I promise.'

'Ok,' she said. 'Well you better come in for a cup of tea.'

'What about social distancing?' I asked.

'Oh, to hell with it,' she said. 'I can't keep up with all these bloody guidelines anyway. I think you're allowed in, if we call it a support bubble.'

'Do I still get a cup of tea in this support bubble?' I asked.

'You sure do.' Ma replied.

We sat there and shot the breeze over me arl Fella. It seemed they'd moved him back into the stroke ward and she'd even been allowed a visit. Although she warned me not to get my hopes up. In the end, I left her waiting on a phone call from the nurse, but I must admit it was lovely to be able to go inside and see her. It's funny that you don't realise how important the little things are until they're gone. As I cycled off up the hill, I began to wonder if the little things in life were really the big things and that all the other stuff was just needless distraction.

My next stop was the allotment. I only went there to rake away the stones and admire my arl Fella's rosebush, which had properly come into bloom by now. But I had hoped I might get word from ar Kenny. After all, it was the last time I'd actually heard him. I say heard, I'd practically caught him red-handed, throwing stones off the *auld* shed roof. He thought I didn't know it was him, the little *blert*.

Sadly, other than the fresh layer of stones, he was nowhere to be seen. So after a quick tidy, I nipped to the supermarket to stock up on supplies. By now, I'd pretty much used all my surplus benefits, although I still had a twenty-grand betting slip sat in my apartment, which as far as I was concerned was mine now. I'd paid that debt in blood.

I was still a little sore as I did my shopping, but I wasn't going to let them get me down. That way they'd won. Once I'd loaded up, I went about my rounds. I had a couple of drops in Dingle, where they *play tick with atchets* and one not far from *der Smithie*. Then it was on to see Graham and Sandy.

I caught them both together when I arrived. Talking across the street from their front steps. 'How's it going?' Graham asked. 'I'm not sure your lot deserve the guard of honour tonight.'

That's the first time I realised he was a City fan. 'If I'd have known you were one of them, I wouldn't have brought your shopping,' I laughed.

'With everything going on, I had to keep it quiet this season,' he said. 'But I'm not one of those glory hunters, I've been a fan since I was a boy.'

'Maybe I'll let you off, then.' I smiled.

'I saw them go down in sixty-three and watched them work their way back up to the top. Back then we had proper players like Summerbee, Bowles and Franny Lee.'

'They were a great team back then,' I said. 'Nothing like the bunch of mercenaries you've got playing for you today.'

'Oh, you're just jealous you couldn't keep hold of Sterling,' he said, smiling.

'And you're just jealous you couldn't hold onto the league,' I replied.

We both laughed. Although at one point I thought Sandy was going to come between us. That was the thing about football, which I'm not sure every woman understands. Sure, I know many of them *Judys* love the game too, but without football, I don't think men would have anything to talk about. Other than *auld* movies of course. But I'd have died of boredom if I had to hear one more story about some *antwacky* film with James Dean or Humphrey Bogart.

I left their shopping on the step and continued on my way. I was desperate to see Pastor McTominay, hoping he'd even throw a couple of blessings our way. But first I wanted to enjoy the fresh air. So I took my bicycle with its empty basket around the city. I thought back to that night before I called Richie for help. It was that awful evening I suddenly realised what a fine city Liverpool was. So I'd made myself a promise to enjoy it more often. Just like on my arl Fella's allotment, today was a beautiful day to smell the roses.

I swung past *der arl Madge*, *der Ippy* and *der Black House* and ate my lunch at the docks *where the bugs wore clogs*. I'd kept myself a little something from my shopping trip and made a proper picnic out of it. With plenty of time until kick-off, I went and bought a posy of flowers and swung past Toxteth Cemetery, as a gift for ar Kenny. I still felt bad that I hadn't caught up with him in ages.

I must've covered nearly ten miles when I finally arrived at the church. I was pretty saddle-sore by then and I staggered like John Wayne as I entered. I laughed, realising how Graham's *antwacky* movies were rubbing off on me. 'Are you alright?' Pastor McTominay, asked as he greeted me by the door.

249

'I'm fine,' I said, suddenly feeling a little drowsy. 'Why do you ask?'

'It's just your speech is a little slurred and you're walking a bit funny.'

'I'll be fine,' I said. 'I just need a cuppa tea and a long sit down.'

Chapter 23

Susan Kennedy

2nd July 2020

As always, I'd been waiting hours for the phone to ring that morning. I'd even mentally prepared myself for the news. I knew it wouldn't make it any easier when it came, but I'd tried to at least steady myself. Usually, I received my daily update between nine and ten, once the nurse had finished her morning rounds, but I was always up long before that. Sleep was something I'd struggled with since Kenny died. It's not that I couldn't get to sleep. It's just at some point or other, I would wake up. After that I could never get back off. Whilst I know it sounds silly, I wondered if I'd had a full night's sleep for thirty years.

I usually just got up and started pottering around, trying not to disturb Ezzy or Lozzle. Even though the house was empty now, old habits died hard. I still got out of bed really quietly to make a cup of tea. It was then I saw ar Wayne at the window. It was a lovely surprise. So with Richie gone, I invited him in. I did wonder if he'd been back on the sauce though, he looked pretty beaten up. He made some lame excuse about falling off his bicycle, which I knew was utter rubbish, but I didn't want to push it. After all, it was lovely he kept popping round to see me, particularly seeing how busy he'd been during lockdown.

In the end, he was pretty keen to get on with his deliveries and I was nervously awaiting that call, so I let him go without interrogation. It was probably only eight-thirty when the phone rang. I knew it was a little strange to get the call so early. *Here we go*, I thought as I picked up the receiver. 'Hi, is that Susan?' the nurse said.

'It's me,' I replied, my voice trembling. 'You're a bit early today, is everything ok?'

'It's not just ok,' she replied. 'Your husband is awake.'

Now, I heard perfectly what she'd said. Only my mind was struggling to process the word *awake*, just as my body struggled to process sleep. 'Sorry, can you say that again?'

'I said, your husband is awake,' the nurse repeated herself, only this time more slowly.

'When?' I asked, frantically. 'How?'

'It must've happened sometime last night,' she said. 'Obviously he's been through one hell of an ordeal and he's slurring his words a little, but he's just about talking if you want to visit him.'

'I'm on my way,' I replied.

I didn't even pack a bag. I just grabbed my phone and my keys and ran straight out the door. I couldn't manage to get hold of either of the boys. I guessed ar Wayne was still on his bicycle and Richie's phone was always busy now the football had started back up. But I did leave a message with Lozzle. I knew she must've been at work and I wondered if they might grant her a visit too, but I wasn't going to push it. This was my chance to see him after five long months and I wasn't ready to share him right away. Not even with my kids.

I'd left the house in such a hurry, I'd completely forgotten my mask. I knew I wasn't allowed on the bus without one, so in the end I called a cab. Thankfully, the nurse on reception gave me a mask when I arrived and she even walked me up to the Stroke Ward, once I told her who I was. It seemed ar Ezzy had become a bit of a local celebrity. Nobody had spent longer in the *ozzy* with the coronavirus than him and he was the only one to recover after such a prolonged battle with the illness. It didn't surprise me. That son of a shipbuilder was as hard as iron and as charming as a puppy. He probably had them all waiting on him hand and foot already.

I couldn't believe it when I saw him lying there. He looked pretty dishevelled. But he was awake, my gorgeous husband, wide awake. 'How are you?' I asked, desperate to take my mask off and kiss him, but I didn't. I definitely didn't want to get thrown out, so I just held his hand instead.

'I've had better mornings,' he replied, in that sweet honey voice of his.

'Well, I haven't,' I said, with tears streaming down my face.

'How are the kids?' he asked.

'Lozzle is fine,' I said. 'She's at work at the moment and they haven't even let her visit you. But I wouldn't be surprised if they make an exception later. She's been so busy helping people with this virus. It's got so much worse since March, but I guess I don't have to tell you that.'

'I don't know.' He smiled. 'I must have slept right through it.'

'You could sleep through anything,' I replied.

'How's Wayne?' he asked.

'He's doing great,' I said, proudly. 'He's been looking after your allotment and donating the proceeds to the church. Pastor McTominay told me he'd also been doing deliveries for people who've been struggling to get out.'

'Ar Wayne?' Ezzy laughed.

'Yep, Pastor McTominay described him as a chip off the old block.'

'Did he now?' Ezzy said. 'Well, we have started to look pretty similar.'

'Not anymore,' I said.

'What do you mean?' Ezzy asked.

'Well, don't take this the wrong way but you look like death warmed up. And as for ar Wayne. Since he's cut out the drinking and started cycling, he looks twenty years younger.'

'That's amazing,' Ezzy replied. 'And Richie, is he back?'

'Back?' I said. 'He even moved in with me for three months. It was lovely to have him home, even if we did drive each other crazy. But he's back at the *Plaza* now. Between you and me, I think he's got a new girlfriend.'

'So him and Mags never worked it out then?' Ezzy asked.

'Nope,' I replied. 'And a good job too if you ask me. I like this new one a lot better, she reminds me of ar Kenny's girlfriend, what was her name?'

'Melody,' Ezzy replied, and then we both went quiet.

'Sorry,' I said. 'I didn't mean to mention Kenny.'

'It's okay,' Ezzy said. 'He'll always be a part of us.'

'I know,' I replied. 'I just miss him every step of the way.'

'He'd be so happy right now. Liverpool are finally champions once more.'

'Who told you?' I asked.

'One of the nurses,' he said.

'Oh, I bet they've all got their eye on you haven't they. You smooth bastard.'

We both laughed, until Ezzy started coughing. Then there was this long uncomfortable silence. We probably had a lot to get off our chests, but neither of us knew where to start. 'Look, there's something I need to say,' we said in unison. 'You, first,' Ezzy added. 'Did you realise I came to visit you last week?' I stuttered, nervously. 'I wanted to tell you, it wasn't your fault.'

'I blamed myself for many years,' Ezzy said. 'That's why I used to spend all my time at my allotment. I couldn't face you.'

'Well, the blame stops now,' I said. 'I realised I never asked you what actually happened. Even now, I still don't want to know. I can only imagine how long you must've stayed there, searching.'

'I'm glad you were spared that ordeal,' he said. 'But in the end, it was just an accident. Like the sinking of the Titanic. Sure people made mistakes. Some of them were down to arrogance and some were down to negligence. But nobody set out to kill anybody that day. You were right to fight for justice, I understand somebody has to be accountable. I think the cover up was criminal, the way they tried to blame us. But really, what is justice when it comes to losing our boy. An eye for an eye?'

'You're right,' I said. 'I think the fighting was my allotment. I couldn't bear the fact you blamed yourself. I thought if I could find someone else to take responsibility, I could spare you that burden. I thought I could get you back. In the end, I just spared you of a wife.'

'No, you didn't,' Ezzy said. 'You were, and always will be, my brown-eyed girl.'

'And you will always be my sweet-talking Preacher man,' I said. 'Whilst you were in here, I started thinking about it as a road we've been walking together. Slowly leaving ar Kenny to rest in peace, whilst we tried to carry on. It's just you made that road look so much easier than I did. I realise now it's because you're stronger than I am.'

'I'm no stronger than you,' Ezzy said. 'I just wasn't walking away from Kenny. With my belief in God, I was walking towards him.'

'I can see that now,' I replied.

'That's why I need you to promise me a couple of things,' Ezzy added. 'Firstly, whether I'm beside you or not, I need you to dance whenever you hear Brown-Eyed Girl.'

'Even if it's playing somewhere in public?' I asked.

'Especially, if it's playing somewhere in public.' He smiled.

'And the other thing?' I asked, already fearing what he was about to say.

'I need you to try and find your faith. Not just in me, but in God. Only then will you be waiting for me and Kenny at the end of the road.'

'I don't know, Ezzy,' I said. 'But I can promise to try.'

Just then Lozzle arrived in her uniform. 'Hi, Dad,' she cried. 'I can't stop, but I was desperate to see you.'

'Well, hold still then,' Ezzy said. 'I want to take a picture of you in my mind.'

'Oh don't be daft,' Lozzle said. 'But make sure you get my best side, if you have to.'

'You've only got best sides,' Ezzy said. He hadn't lost any of his smoothness.

'Ma, can I have a word?' Lozzle said, turning towards me.

'Sure, go ahead, luv.' I replied.

'No, I mean can I have a word outside,' she said, suddenly looking all serious.

I followed her out into the corridor. 'What is it?'

'It's ar Wayne,' she replied.

Chapter 24
Richie Kennedy
2nd July 2020

I'd been watching the football when Lozzle called. I wasn't that bothered about the intrusion. Of course I'd celebrated when we became champions, but this was a total anti-climax. After giving us a guard of honour, City were now treating us to a good old-fashioned thumping. What a way to come crashing back down to Earth. 'Richie,' she said and even then I knew it was bad news.

'Is it the arl Fella?' I asked.

'No, He's actually awake,' she replied.

'He's awake?' I said, not quite able to believe it. 'When?'

'Late last night,' Lozzle replied, but she still sounded deflated.

'When can I see him?' I asked.

'Soon, Richie. But I've got bad news.'

'Just come out with it,' I said, fearing he had brain damage or something. When it came to bad news, I always preferred the *Band-Aid* method of just ripping the plaster straight off.

'It's Wayne,' she replied. 'It seems he's had a massive brain haemorrhage from a beating he took a few days ago. Pastor McTominay found him outside the church.'

'Wayne, at church?' I said, totally confused. 'I don't understand.'

'Me neither,' she replied. 'I just need you to get a few bits from his place, pyjamas and stuff and meet me in intensive care. I've cleared it with the Matron, she says you can visit as long as you bring your mask.'

That's the moment I realised it was serious. After all, my arl Fella had been on death's door for months and nobody had been allowed to visit him. My head was spinning at ninety miles an hour. He was awake, but now something had happened to Wayne. Thank God that car of mine could practically drive itself, otherwise I wouldn't have made it to ar Wayne's. I didn't have a spare key to get in, which made me feel awful. My own brother and I didn't even have the keys to his flat. Thankfully, Pastor McTominay had left a set with a neighbour, who handed them on to me. I was glad he didn't stick around. I just wanted to be alone.

I looked around ar Wayne's place. It was nothing how I imagined. There were no take-way boxes or empty beer cans. It was immaculate. Beside his bed were two pieces of paper. The first was the betting slip, still yet to be cashed in. What a waste I thought. He clearly had the money to pay off his debts, only they must've caught him unawares and taken the debt in blood. Fucking animals. I wished he'd just let me pay them off. But even I had to admit that fighting had brought us back together. We'd proper won that one. He was the hardest man I knew, ar Wayne. Other than my arl Fella, of course.

Still, that debt was paid now, as far as I was concerned. So I carefully put the betting slip in my pocket, hoping it might bring Wayne some good fortune at the *ozzy*. According to Lozzle, it was Pastor McTominay who'd found him. So obviously ar Wayne had been making good during lockdown. It was just a shame this had to happen, especially now, just as my arl Fella had woken up. I wondered if Ma knew. I guessed she did. I suppose she must have been at the *auld* man's bedside. The whole situation was a total mess.

It was then I picked up the other piece of paper. The note. There was a date at the top, so I worked out when he had written it. By the looks of things, it must've been the night he'd called me.

He'd obviously thought about killing himself. I was so grateful he hadn't, but still I felt guilty it had come to that before he called. He must've spent all those years blaming himself for Kenny. I'd never really analysed it before, but those three years between us clearly made a world of difference. Whilst I'd run away from it all, he had stayed, drowning in the sorrow of what could've been. It had obviously weighed him down far more than I'd imagined.

Being older than Kenny, he felt responsible, whereas I hadn't blamed anyone. I put it down as a horrible accident, followed by a disgusting cover up, but rather than wallowing in it, I'd moved on.

In many ways it was a beautiful thing, that letter. But I knew Ma shouldn't read it. It would only upset her. So I folded it up for safe-keeping and stuffed it in my pocket with the betting slip. I picked up a bag and threw in ar Wayne's Liverpool pyjamas and some shaving stuff and locked the door behind me. I don't know why I was in such a rush to leave. I just had the feeling time was of the essence.

It was pretty empty at the *ozzy*, the numbers of patients with the virus had fallen, for now at least. There was even a spare nurse to walk me down to Intensive Care. Lozzle was there beside the bed when I arrived and helped me unpack Wayne's things. 'I hope it wasn't that fight we had with those two *meff*s outside the bookies,' I said.

'It wasn't,' Lozzle replied. 'Pastor McTominay told me it was the night City lost to Chelsea.'

'Oh,' I said. 'I hadn't realised Wayne had been going to church.'

'Me neither,' Lozzle said. 'But Ma told me he'd been donating the arl Fella's vegetables to the food bank.'

'I knew that much,' I replied. 'But it seems he'd really turned things around this time.'

'Yeah,' Lozzle said, trying to hide her tears, but failing miserably.

'I hadn't realised he'd blamed himself for ar Kenny,' I said. 'That's what all the drinking and gambling was about.'

Lozzle just rolled her eyes. 'For God's sake, Richie. I know you've been in London for the past three decades, but it isn't bloody Mars.'

'I know,' I said and I just threw my arms around her. 'Sometimes we can't see what's right in front of ar noses.'

'You can say that again,' she replied.

'Which reminds me,' I said. 'That Amber isn't ar Kenny's girl after all.'

'I know,' she said. 'But let's not talk about it now.'

'Agreed,' I said, pulling us both up a chair beside Wayne's bed.

We sat there in silence for what might've been hours, listening to the beep of the heart-rate monitor and the sound of the ventilator going up and down. I knew it was a bad sign when nobody asked us to leave at the end of visiting hours. We waited until the blue sky outside faded into an aching grey. Ar Lozzle drifted off first. I couldn't blame her. I think she'd started off that morning at work, so she must have been absolutely knackered.

Alone in the darkness, I took out the betting slip and shoved it into ar Wayne's hand. I tightened his loose fingers around it and I was about to read the letter to him, when I heard ar Kenny's voice. 'Don't worry,' he said. 'I'll take care of him now.'

I looked to Lozzle to see if she'd heard it too, but just at that moment the little machine stopped beeping and let out one awful flat tone. She instantly woke up and ran for the Doctor. But I think we both knew it was too late.

Just like that. Wayne was gone.

Chapter 25

Ezra Kennedy

2nd July 2020

I was having that dream again, only I was no longer confused what time it was. It was the second of July in the year twenty-twenty of Our Lord. The ageing stones of the auld buildings beside the water were the giveaway and the low sun told me it was late. By now, the only thing stuck in the passage of time was that giant boat beside the quayside. Her black hull glistened like freshly laid tar and her fairy lights sparkled as if it were her maiden voyage.

The streets behind remained lined with well-wishers, only now they were members of my congregation. My boys were by my side too, but this time our tickets said *First Class* and we were the only ones trying to get onboard. Which gave us plenty of time to savour the view. It was lovely to get one last look of Liverpool, the place which had become my home. I even caught sight of Susan waving us off on our way.

It was a magical experience, when we finally drifted out into the sunset, with her chimney stacks puffing out thick plumes of smoke and her engines humming a baritone roar. This time we were welcomed to the upper decks, to sit with those finely dressed gentlemen. But much to our surprise, they partied like the paupers down below. Beer was flowing from their china cups and songs were being sung. Before long, the tables were pushed aside, as people chose to dance along too. I hadn't noticed until then, but my boys were older than before, old enough to drink. So I accompanied them in a crafty one, before we joined in with the fun.

We all linked arms and swayed merrily, as the fiddlers played a tune. I remember wishing that dance could go on a while longer, but it ended right on time. Five minutes and as many seconds to be exact. That's when we hit something with an almighty thud. But this time we stayed together, holding each other's hands. Wayne and Richie seemed to know exactly what to do, like they'd practiced it before. It was ar Kenny who looked surprised, until I turned to him and said, 'As if you didn't know that was coming.'

That giant old lady began to dip below the waves once more, but nobody panicked. Least of all me. Gravity seemed to have no bearing, as if our bodies no longer had weight. We just carried on dancing, without a care in the world. Those fiddlers managed to hold their places too and they continued to play a tune for us. Just like before. Still, I felt guilty as hell when we finally got to the front and our lifeboat was cut free. After all, we were the only ones onboard.

We bobbed back into the harbour, where Susan and Lauren were waiting for us. Susan reached out a hand and helped ar Richie to shore, then she turned to me and said, 'I just wanted you to know it wasn't your fault, Ezzy. I never blamed you, not for one minute.'

'I know, my wild rose,' I replied and I opened my arms and gave her one last hug. One last kiss. I did the same to Lauren before I turned to Richie. 'No sloping back to London this time. You're the man of the house now.'

Then Wayne, Kenny and I turned that lifeboat around and went back towards that sinking ship, to see how many of those souls we could save. We needn't have bothered to hurry though. That ship was no longer floundering when we found her. Somehow, she'd risen from her watery grave, like the Son of our Holy Father, like the sun above us. It was morning already. The sky was now blue and nobody was in a rush to get back on board. They'd stayed in the water, clinging to old tables and pulled their chairs on top. Decorated with red scarfs, a floating party was about to begin. So we dropped anchor and joined them. We knew we'd have to get back aboard that ship eventually. When that time came, we even knew where she would take us. She was headed home, to reunite us with my father, but we weren't going to miss this party. We'd waited thirty years for this one.

Chapter 26
Richie Kennedy
15th July 2020

In many ways I'd spent the past three months preparing myself for the news that my arl Fella had died. All I can tell you is it didn't make it any easier. It was both a strange and terrible coincidence that he passed away a few hours after ar Wayne. After all, he'd only just woke up and I didn't even get the chance to see him. But at least they both had someone beside them when it happened.

I never asked Ma exactly how he went, but I know the broad brush strokes. Although he'd risen from his coma and fought off the illness bravely, his body was just too weak. The fact he'd regained consciousness defied all logic. Maybe he was just so determined to set things straight between himself and Ma, that he found away. Who knows. All I do know was his cause of death read much the same as my brother Wayne's. They both suffered a massive bleed on the brain. The doctors said neither would have felt any pain and it would have taken them both almost instantly.

That was some comfort at least, although nobody wanted to say it to Ma. To be honest, nobody knew what to say to her. She'd suffered enough in her life after the loss of Kenny, but to lose another son and a husband in one day, just seemed worse than cruel. It was brutal. Of course, I moved back home and so did Lozzle. Despite the virus still being around, she was granted long-term leave. To be honest, I wondered if she'd ever go back after what she'd been through over the course of this virus.

We took turns keeping douse over Ma, but over the next few days the *auld gerl* surprised us really. She often looked quiet or reflective, she wouldn't eat much and she obviously didn't say a lot. But under the circumstances, she seemed to be holding up remarkably well. 'At least I got to say goodbye to Ezzy,' she kept saying. Neither Lozzle or I doubted how important it was, we just couldn't help but wonder whether she'd even begun to process the loss of ar Wayne yet. Still, it was early days and we were both just amazed that her legs could still hold her weight. She was a miracle ar Ma.

One night, on one of my trips to the fridge, I found her asking *Alexa* to play Brown Eyed Girl. At least I had my clothes on this time. Still, I coughed to alert her to my attention. If I hadn't known better, I would've even said I'd caught her dancing. 'Are you alright, Ma?' I asked.

'As alright as I could be,' she replied. 'I promised Ezra, I'd dance to this whenever I heard it. I was just getting some practice in.'

'You're doing bloody amazing if you ask me,' I said.

'Promise me, you'll get some sleep, though. Won't you?'

'There's some things that can't be promised,' Ma replied. 'I've promised Ezzy to dance when I hear that song. I've promised him to try and find my faith. I'm not sure about that one, but I've agreed to help Pastor McTominay by becoming a Church Elder. What I really need is for you to promise me something.'

'Anything, Ma,' I said. 'Just tell me what you need.'

'I want you to come back home,' she said. 'You can do your work from anywhere and you've got that lovely new lass up here now.'

'As soon as the sale of the flat goes through.' I said. 'I promise to stay. But I think we both know it's for the best if I buy my own place up here.'

'Agreed,' Ma said. Then she turned *Alexa* back on and we danced together in the darkness of the kitchen.

I tried to make as many of the arrangements as possible. With coronavirus restrictions, we were only going to be allowed a small gathering at my arl Fella's church. Pastor McTominay took care of most of the minor details. We didn't mind about the numbers. To be honest, we just wanted family to be present, along with a few well-wishers from my arl Fella's congregation. Ma insisted in keeping with Irish traditions, pretty much forcing us to hold a wake. So on the third day, she kicked both me and Lozzle out to the local pub to arrange it. Lozzle had planned to meet Giles there, who'd flown in specially from the Isle of Man. Of course I didn't mind, I even offered him my hotel room at the *Plaza*.

'Hey, Lozzle,' I said, on the way over. 'I hope you don't mind, but I've invited Amber to join us too,' I said.

'Amber?' Lozzle, replied. 'Why the hell would you invite her?'

It was then I realised, with everything going on, I hadn't told her. 'I know she's not ar niece,' I said. 'Which is probably a good thing, seeing as she's now my girlfriend.'

Lozzle didn't look impressed, 'Since when?' she asked.

'It's been a couple of weeks,' I said. 'I know you're not overly keen on her, but the whole mix up was my fault really. I hadn't told her when Kenny died. Once she found out, it was her who set the record straight.'

Lozzle looked at me sternly. 'Ok, Rich,' she said. 'I'll give her a chance for your sake. But if she takes advantage of you, then God help her.'

I smiled. I knew it would take a while for Lozzle to warm to her. But she had the best intentions when it came to ar family. In that way, she was just like Ma.

It was a weird experience when we arrived at the pub. Partly because Amber and Giles had already arrived and sat down at a table. To everyone else they must've looked like a couple, after all, they were both ridiculously attractive and about the same age. I tugged on ar Lozzle's sleeve as we approached. 'You've got to admit, we've both done pretty well, there.'

She just smiled. I say, *just*, it was a beautiful thing to witness. Particularly with the events of the past few days. The other thing I noticed as we sat down was how much pubs had changed. We had to fill out little cards with ar names and addresses on them, so the government could track us if there were any reported cases of coronavirus. It wasn't a big deal, but I couldn't help but feel this was the beginning of the end for the local boozer. Popular people mixed with their friends online, in *WhatsApp* groups and on *Facebook*. Whilst of course they would meet up, from time to time, more often than not pubs were a place for loners. People like ar Wayne. People like him could get rubbing shoulders at the bar with similar folk and start talking about football. Or in ar Wayne's case, start fighting over football. But now you had to stay on your own table and these loners just remained alone. I don't know if it was just all the emotions of the past few days spilling out, but it brought a tear to my eye. 'Wayne would've hated this,' I said. 'Not being able to go up to the bar.'

Lozzle nodded in agreement. 'Yeah, he would,' she said. 'But that was the *auld* Wayne. You know he'd stopped drinking by the end.'

'Completely stopped?' I asked.

'So Ma says,' Lozzle added.

'We can't have the wake somewhere like here,' I said. 'It just doesn't feel right.'

'I've got an idea,' Giles said, interrupting. 'I hope you don't mind me suggesting it?'

'No, please,' I replied. 'Go ahead.'

'Well, Lozzle mentioned your arl Fella had an allotment and that Wayne had spent his last few days there. Giving out vegetables to the needy,' Giles said. 'So why don't we hold the wake there. We could set up a couple of barrels in the shed and with it being outdoors, it would be far safer.'

'I love it,' Lozzle said, squeezing his arm tightly.

'Me too,' I said looking across to Amber, who had been very quiet. I realised she must've been wary of Lozzle.

'Have you thought about music for the funeral,' she said, bravely.

'Ma's got ar arl Fella sorted,' Lozzle replied. 'But I still haven't got a clue what they should play for Wayne.'

'Something to do with Liverpool Football Club?' Giles asked.

'That's very kind of you, as a blue-nose,' Lozzle joked.

'But I really want something which captures who he was and how much he'd pulled it around in those last few weeks.'

'What about *A Change Is Gonna Come*,' Amber said. 'By Sam Cooke.'

Lozzle looked thoughtful for a moment. 'I love it,' she said and smiled.

I took Amber's hand beneath the table. I knew it was still early days and I knew ar family had been through something of a storm recently, but right there, I also realised there was hope. After all, it poured with rain most of the time on Merseyside, but we all knew it couldn't rain forever.

It seemed Ma had been out too when we got home. She'd been over to the allotment and cut a giant bunch of roses to add to all the flowers which had been delivered over the previous few days. 'These ones are for the coffins,' she said and then she finally gave in and sobbed her eyes out. We both comforted her, Lozzle and I. But it wasn't easy. The following day she kicked us out again to go and clear out Wayne's flat.

I still didn't let anybody know about the letter. But we all agreed the money from his betting slip should go to a good cause. It must've taken all of five seconds to decide on the Hillsborough Family Support Group. It took a lot longer to tidy up the rest of Wayne's affairs. His flat wasn't messy, but it was a treasure trove of *auld* photographs and memories. There was a shoe-box of pictures which Lozzle's said Wayne had showed her recently. That's where she'd found the drawing of Kenny the clown.

I found this lovely *auld* picture of Kenny's football team, the year he scored sixty-two. The frame was broken and the glass was cracked, but I put it to one side, knowing it was an easy fix and that Ma would treasure it. But it was nothing compared to what ar Lozzle found under his bed. That blew us both away. 'Well, I'll be damned,' she said, pulling it out from a pile of magazines.

'What is it?' I asked, noticing something red and fluffy in her hand.

'It's a wig,' she replied.

'Maybe Wayne used to wear it at the football?' I asked.

'Nope,' Lozzle said. 'I know exactly where I've seen it before.'

'He didn't dress up as a woman did he?' I joked.

'Nope. It's from his Kenny the clown outfit,' she giggled, pulling out a flared pair of trousers and a baggy Liverpool shirt. 'All those years I thought it was my imagination. And it was actually ar Wayne.'

'It must've been his way of making sure you got to know your other brother,' I said.

'The big daft bugger,' she replied, with tears now streaming down her cheeks. 'That's obviously why he'd kept my Kenny the clown picture. He probably didn't want to let on it was him because of all the trouble it caused.'

'What to Nan's trifle?' I said. 'God rest her soul.' Now we were both laughing and crying. It was hard, reducing ar big brother's life to two piles of *keep* and *throw*. But just like our laughter through the tears, it was worth it.

It was a Wednesday when the funerals finally took place, on a rare but beautiful sunny day in Liverpool. Despite the fact only thirty were allowed in the church, Wayne and ar arl Fella got a guard of honour of their own, as hundreds decided to line the streets for their arrival. We were all taken aback. The only thing we were worried about was somebody mentioning Hillsborough. Both Lozzle and I decided it was not to be spoken of all day. We argued over this next point. But in the end, we agreed that she would remain at Ma's side all day, so I could deal with the undertakers and the guests.

With social-distancing, I wasn't even allowed to carry the coffins. I understood the reasons behind it, after all, we were from separate households to the pallbearers. But it was still a shame to miss out on the honour of carrying the man and brother who'd carried me their entire lives on their final journey. I had wanted Giles alongside me too, it would've been nice to involve him, as he was pretty much one of the family now. But it wasn't meant to be.

In the end, they brought the *auld* man inside to *Into the Mystic* by Van Morrison. We all knew Ma would pick a song by *Van the Man,* but we'd all expected Brown-Eyed Girl. I couldn't deny the lyrics of this one fitted better, especially the final line. Wayne followed him in to *A Change is Gonna Come*, and I looked across to Amber and sent her a grateful nod. By then there wasn't a dry eye in the room.

Pastor McTominay took the service, standing at the lectern and reading the Parable of the Sower, just as my Ma had requested.

Listen! Behold, a sower went out to sow. And as he sowed, some seed fell along the path, and the birds came and devoured it. Other seed fell on rocky ground, where it did not have much soil, and immediately it sprang up, since it had no depth of soil. And when the sun rose, it was scorched, and since it had no root, it withered away. Other seed fell among thorns, and the thorns grew up and choked it, and it yielded no grain. And other seeds fell into good soil and produced

278

grain, growing up and increasing and yielding thirtyfold and sixtyfold and a hundredfold." And he said, "He who has ears to hear, let him hear."

Mark 4:3-9

Then it was my turn to speak. I hadn't written anything down, I was worried my hands would be shaking too much to read from anything. 'I know Pastor McTominay would tell you the parable of the sower was about a Preacher and his congregation's search for faith,' I said, my voice wavering a little under the strain. 'And I'm sure my arl Fella would agree. But knowing Ezra, or Ezzy, as my Ma always called him, he'd have probably had his own take on things. He'd probably tell you it was also about grief. He might tell you that mine and Lauren's grief had somehow landed on good soil, and in many ways he'd be right. He might tell you that ar Wayne's grief and my Ma's grief had landed amongst the thorns. Thankfully, they were both strong enough to grow through it. But that's not how I like to think of grief. I like to think back to that sunny holiday we had beside the sea. The one where my arl Fella's car broke down at the gates to Pontins. I remember plenty of laughter on that holiday. Kenny dressing up as a clown for the adult's fancy dress party. But most of the laughter was aimed at me, when I got stung by a bee on the beach.' I paused, worried I might've

279

gone too far mentioning Kenny, after all, we'd agreed not to talk about Hillsborough. Thankfully, even Ma was laughing as she snivelled. 'I remember shouting for somebody to call the police. I don't know how old I was, but even then I knew it wasn't a police matter when you got stung by a bee. But what people didn't understand is that I have a rare condition. I get this strange reaction from bee stings. Every time I get stung, every bee sting I've ever had swells up too. That's how I suffer grief. And let's just say, I can feel a few bee-stings today.'

I sat back down and took my seat. I knew I hadn't spoken for long, but it felt like an hour. Ma was blubbing into her hanky and ar Lozzle was stroking her on the arm. I wished I'd said more about my brother, but we'd agreed that Lozzle would take that burden from my shoulders, just as the pallbearers had when they carried him in. With all my bee-stings playing up and my eyes watering, part of me was relieved it was over.

Chapter 27

Susan Kennedy

15th July 2020

Without looking at a calendar, I couldn't tell you how many days there were between them dying and the funeral. Those days seemed to last forever. I remember Richie and Lozzle bringing me endless cups of tea. The telly was pretty much always on, showing one game of football after another. I usually like a good game, but I couldn't even concentrate on which team was which. In the end, I had to kick them both out to go and organise the wake. I pretended it was some great Irish tradition of ar Ezzy's, but truthfully I was willing to suffer another couple of hours of pain that day, in exchange for some peace on this one. The moment they'd gone, I missed them. I realised it wasn't them making me feel claustrophobic, it was the four walls. So I popped out to Ezzy's allotment and took a few cuttings from his rosebush.

I know that every day is the same length. Twenty-four hours or one-thousand, four-hundred and forty minutes to be precise. But that day of the funeral was undoubtedly the longest day of my life. I always had trouble sleeping, but usually I'd get a bit of shut-eye before I woke up tossing and turning. That night I didn't sleep at all. I remember rolling over towards my alarm clock at the stroke of midnight and thinking, *it's already started.*

Even though it wasn't one of those old-fashioned clocks which ticked, I must've counted down every second until I eventually gave up any hope of sleep at about four. It was then I got out of bed and put my rollers in my hair. Lozzle had already ironed my outfit. I wish she hadn't. I was desperate for something to do and the thought of removing the creases from my dress was about as therapeutic as it got. Instead, I just pottered around the house until the kids got up. I say kids, Lozzle was nearly thirty and Richie was forty-five. But like any mother will tell you, they'll always be my babies. Of course I made them both breakfast, despite their protests. 'It's what mothers do,' I said. But other than that, there wasn't much for me to distract myself with that morning.

They both wolfed down their eggs and bacon, even though they claimed they weren't that hungry. Of course, I couldn't stomach a thing. I couldn't even hold down a cup of tea. Richie had arranged everything and the funeral cars picked us up with more than enough time to spare. We were in one of those limousines with two rows of seats. Giles and Amber were already in the front row. I was glad to see them. It was nice both my kids had someone special in their lives.

It was a beautiful sight as we drove up to church. It was a blue-skied afternoon, without a cloud in the sky, but I couldn't believe just how many people had turned out to show their faces. Shame on me, but I didn't recognise half of them. That was something I was going to have to put right once this awful day was over. They probably knew ar Ezzy, after all he'd helped so many people over the years through the Church. But I'd like to think some of them were there for ar Wayne too. The local paper had done a double-page spread on his tragic death and his support for others during coronavirus. They had asked me for a comment, but I declined. I did give them my blessing to run the story though. I wanted people to remember ar Wayne for the good he did, not for the alcoholic he'd become for so many years after Kenny died.

The hardest part of the day was stepping into the Church. I knew there was no turning back after that. I also knew that nobody expected me to get up and talk. But those who were there, my family and my closest friends, probably realised they wouldn't be able to stop me. The songs to bring them both in couldn't have been better. Obviously, I'd chosen Ezzy's. I laid a single bloom of his red rose on his coffin. So together, we could magnificently float into the mystic. Father McTominay was a real help that day too and I thought ar

Richie spoke beautifully. He got that perfect balance between sorrow and joy. We were all crying. But as my Ezzy would've said, they were a rainbow of tears.

Still, I wondered if my legs would carry me up to the altar. Ar Lozzle had tried to accompany me, but I'd shrugged her off. I wasn't being rude, but this section of the difficult path was mine to walk alone. There were a few murmurs in the audience and I knew what they were thinking, *how the hell was this woman still standing?* Well, only God knew the answer to that.

'Hello,' I said, starting bravely. 'Thank you all for coming and send my thanks to those who couldn't make it. These are difficult times for all of us.' I paused to take a sip of water. 'I know you all thought I might not speak. I also know that everybody has been instructed not to mention Hillsborough. Well, I just did. Hillsborough. It was the moment which changed my life. In fact, all our lives as a family. In many ways I lost more than just a son that day. For many years I lost my husband too. I'm just grateful I got the chance to tell ar Ezzy that he wasn't to blame. I wish I could've told Wayne too. But it was ar Ezzy who taught me an important lesson on his final day. He taught me something can be an accident, despite there being people at fault. He compared it to the Titanic. I think we all know a number of reasons why that mighty ship sank, but over time people have let her rest at the bottom of the ocean. Now, I'm not sure I'll ever be able to forgive those people who made the mistakes which robbed me of my son and I'm never going to let it rest at the bottom of an ocean, but I made ar Ezzy a number of promises that day. Some I'm not sure I will be able to keep. But I will promise in front of all of you, to put the same energy I've spent fighting for justice over the past thirty years, into searching for peace. For Ezzy, for Wayne and for the two beautiful children I have left.'

I wasn't sure how people would react at first. Most of them just sat there, slack-jawed. Some could not hold my eyes, as they buried their heads into their handkerchiefs. Then all of a sudden, someone started clapping. I'm not sure who it was. But as I returned to my seat, I returned to a standing ovation. It still didn't make it easy to take those nine or ten steps back to the front row. I still couldn't feel my feet on the floor. But somehow, I must've made it. As I sat back down, part of me wondered if those people clapping had actually carried me.

Chapter 28

Lauren Kennedy

29th July 2020

It was my turn to speak next. I waited for Ma to be seated and for the standing ovation to finish. I realised it wasn't a competition, but I wondered how I would follow that. Nervously, I stood and made a few paces forward to take my place beside my brother Wayne. 'I know a lot of you will remember my brother as somebody who liked a drink, but I'm not sure that's entirely true. You know what they say, a man takes a drink, then the drink takes a drink and, before you know it, the drink takes a man.' I started, nervously. 'But many of you will also know that ar Wayne was a fighter too. Not always in the most positive sense, but in his final few weeks he won his greatest battle of all. He overcame his demons. As many of the kind people who have shown up today will testify, ar Wayne helped hundreds of strangers during lockdown. Taking vegetables from my father's allotment, he spread kindness throughout his beloved city of Liverpool. He went further still, using what little money he had to shop for people who needed it the most. And, in one final act of kindness, he made a very generous donation to a charity very close to his heart. However, I will always remember my big brother as a clown.' I took out the wig I'd been hiding in my bag and rested it on his coffin. 'I only found out after he passed away, but it was Wayne who dressed up as a clown, which he called Kenny. The one I drew on my fifth birthday party, which ended up ruining my Nan's trifle. It was his way of making sure I got to know the brother I never met, in a safe way, in a way without the tragedy. So, in that spirit, that's how I'd like us all to remember Wayne. As a red wig-wearing, Liverpool-loving, clown. But without the tragedy.'

I knew I hadn't spoken for long and I wondered if I'd got it right, but I caught Richie sending me an approving glance as I sat back down next to Ma. She was still crying, but I felt her squeeze my arm and she whispered, 'Well done, *gerl*.'

Pastor McTominay finished up the service with a prayer, 'Give to your whole Church in heaven and on earth your light and your peace. Grant that all who have been nourished by the holy body and blood of your son may be raised to immortality and incorruption to be seated with him at your heavenly banquet.'

Ma stood up and handed each of us a red rose to place on the coffins. Then the two most important men in my life made their final journey. We left the church to Dusty Springfield's *Son of a Preacher Man*. It was Ma's choice, but it was perfect for both of them. I remember her telling me how her and Ezzy had come back up the aisle to *Stuck in the Middle With You,* and I suppose this gave a kind of *Pulp Fiction* symmetry to the *auld* Fella's life. I know he'd have liked that. He was always far too gangster to be a Pastor.

We got back into the funeral cars and travelled to the allotment, which was to become both my arl Fella's and my two brothers' final resting place. Whilst we had a memorial for ar Kenny in the cemetery at Toxteth, Ma had never scattered his ashes, she hadn't known where until now. So on that beautiful afternoon, we laid them to rest, although we all decided the allotment would remain a rose garden from now onwards. Partly because nobody fancied eating vegetables grown in soil where we'd scattered their ashes, but also because of the amazing colour of the flowers growing from my arl Fella's rosebush. It was the brightest red, the colour of Anfield.

Somebody must have also tipped off the other allotment owners because whilst none of them were in attendance, they'd all tied red and white scarfs to their fences and gate posts. It literally looked like the terraces of the Kop. Giles had done a great job too, decking out the shed in tiny fairy lights. As dusk came, it looked amazing, like how I imagined the Titanic must've appeared on her maiden journey. We all lit candles too and had a quiet moment of reflection before the fun began. Richie and Giles had become quite pally and, with a bit of help from Amber, they'd set up a couple of barrels on draft and bought more than a few bottles of wine. Although I think it was Richie who'd rigged up a sound system. It was so high-tech, only he could operate it and he spent half the night playing DJ. Just as Ma had hoped, we had a proper wake for the arl Fella, with Irish music and everything. It wasn't one of those morbid affairs, where people you hardly know keep coming round to shake your hand to say, "Sorry for your loss." It was a proper celebration of their lives, with just a few close friends and family.

Every time Van Morrison came on, Ma would get up and dance, grabbing a different one of us to hold her hand. By the end of the night, we were all knees deep in mud and pretty pissed too.

Then, all of a sudden, Giles nodded to Richie and a slow weepy song came on. Before I knew it, it was just me and Giles dancing, with all the others standing around the edges. At the end of the song, he dropped to one knee in that mud and produced the biggest diamond I'd ever seen. 'Lauren Kennedy,' he said. 'Would you do me the honour of becoming my wife?'

'Are you proposing to me at a double funeral?' I asked, with tears streaming down my face.

'No,' he replied. 'I'm asking here, in the soil where your father worked, because I never got the chance to ask for his blessing. But with everything you've done for other people during this pandemic, I was wondering if I could be the one who takes care of you from now on?'

'Well, you could've asked me on that bloody helicopter of your arl Fella's,' I replied.

'Is that a no?' he said, nervously.

'Of course it's not a no,' I said. 'But I've got one condition.'

'Anything,' he said, his face now lighting up.

'We do it at the arl Fella's church,' I replied.

'It's a deal,' Giles said, standing up and kissing me gently.

Then I kissed him back. Just not a funeral sort of kiss, a proper passionate snog, whilst my whole family watched and cheered. 'You've got yourself all muddy doing it there,' I whispered, as I pulled away. 'Lucky I've still got some bubble bath left. If you've still got the hotel room key?'

'It can be arranged,' Giles said, glancing across to Richie and we both laughed.

Chapter 29
Richie Kennedy
22nd July 2020

During the week of the funeral, I was so busy making arrangements, I hadn't paid much attention to football. Obviously, I was glad we were declared champions in time for my arl Fella and Wayne to see it, but I didn't have a chance to catch any of the games after that thumping at the hands of Man City. By the sounds of things, I didn't miss much. Our form was still a bit patchy, beating Villa and Brighton relatively easily, before dropping two points against Burnley and losing to Arsenal. Not that it really mattered in terms of league position, we were only chasing a few meaningless records by then. But strangely, as the following week came, I suddenly had this overwhelming urge to be there, for Liverpool versus Chelsea. There were still a few games left in the season, but this was the big one. It's where we would receive the league trophy, for the first time in thirty years.

Now, I hadn't been to sit in the stands since Hillsborough, I still didn't like crowded places. I tended to work with my clients in boardrooms and offices. If I was really pushed to go to a game, then I insisted they fork out for a box. However, this one was different, it was behind closed doors.

Nobody was allowed in, except the press, which made it all the more appealing and gave me an incredible idea. I called my old mate Phil from the Echo. I say mate, basically I fed him stories of upcoming transfers in exchange for favours. Still, this was a big ask to get a ticket into Anfield that night.

'Hi Phil, it's Richie,' I said. 'I'm about to call in all those favours you owe me and then some.'

'What do you need, pal?' Phil asked.

'A press pass to Liverpool against Chelsea.'

Phil laughed. 'Don't be daft, I've got freelancers queuing up for that gig.'

'I'll write you a match report, Phil. And I could feed you a tasty little bit of gossip too.'

'Ok, I'm going to level with you,' Phil said. 'Obviously, we've held the back page for the game at Anfield, but I am short of content due to the cancellation of local games. If you could get me a great story, which had a community theme to it, then I might be able to help. It's got to be a big one though. I'm after a double-page spread.'

'Well, it's funny you should mention that Phil,' I said confidently. 'Amber Andrews has just signed for Liverpool Ladies. She's played in the local league all her life and she just saved Merseyrail from relegation with a wonder goal. She's a red through and through, a local girl, and a strong black female with outspoken views on Black Lives Matter. Do you think you could make a story out of that?'

'Depends how much access I could get to her?' Phil asked.

'Full backstage passes, Phil.' I said, shamelessly boasting now. 'She also happens to be my girlfriend.'

'Ok, Richie.' Phil said. 'Swing by the office and I'll get you a press pass for the Chelsea game. But I'm serious about needing a match report. You're putting a freelancer out of work with this one.'

'Understood,' I said, jubilantly. 'Now, I owe you one.'

So that's how I got into Anfield that night. Other than the teams and a few club officials, I was pretty much the only one. After showing my pass, they tried to usher me into the press box, but I told them I wanted to write my article from the missing fans perspective and, in the end, I persuaded them to let me watch the game from the Kop.

The strangest thing happened as I climbed the stairs to walk out into the stands. Maybe it was just an emotional hangover from everything I'd been through over the past few days. Maybe it was because nobody had turned the lights on because they'd expected the stand to be empty. But somewhere, in those dark corridors which led out into the stadium, I caught sight of them. My arl Fella and my brothers. Only they were young again, with their red scarfs on, just like that day at Hillsborough.

The big fella had one arm around ar Kenny and the other sort of resting on Wayne's shoulder. That was the best he could do, seeing as ar Wayne was jumping up and down. He always was a livewire on match day. The first to start dancing and the one to start the chant off in the stands. I went over and joined them, there was something I desperately wanted to say to my arl Fella. 'Hey, Dad,' I said. 'I just wanted you to know it wasn't your fault. I never got the chance to tell you with everything that happened.'

'I know,' he said. 'It doesn't matter now, anyway.'

'In fact there's something I wanted you to have,' I said, pulling out the letter Wayne had written for Ma. 'Keep it safe won't you and don't read it to Ma until you see her again.'

'Of course,' he replied. 'And tell your big brother it wasn't his fault either. I can't seem to get any sense out of him at the moment.'

I joined Wayne on my arl Fella's far right and tried to talk to him, but Wayne, being Wayne, was far too excited to listen. He'd already started singing. 'Walk on, walk on...'

So that's what we did. The four of us, for the first time since Hillsborough. We walked out onto the terraces. Of course by the time I stepped out into the floodlights they were gone. But I could still hear those words coming through the speakers. Only there were hundreds of voices now. 'With hope, in your heart...'

'And you'll never walk alone,' I sang along, at the top of my lungs.

Whilst it was only a recording, I guessed those voices were just as real as my arl Fella's and my brothers had been beside me. They were the voices of people, just like them, who's spirits would remain at the Kop-end, cheering on their team, forever more. Somewhere in the ether, I could even hear the immortal words of Bill Shankly, "Some people believe football is a matter of life and death, I am very disappointed with that attitude. I can assure you it is much, much more important than that."

I think I finally understood what he'd meant. It wasn't just a game. It was tribal. It was belonging to something far bigger than yourself. It was the ritual of a father taking his boys to cheer on their team and teaching them how to become men. It was a family far bigger than your own. I might not have known all their names, but those voices in the crowd were just like ours. They'd probably each suffered their own losses over the past thirty years. It was at that moment, I realised how important it was to be some place, where everybody's troubles were all the same.

It turned out to be one of the greatest games of football I've ever seen. We put five past them that night. Okay, so they might have scored three back, but those goals were irrelevant. Like the three decades I'd spent away. As the ref blew the final whistle, I thought about those thirty years it had taken us to regain the title. I wondered if this current crop were actually as good as the team from the late eighties, which I watched religiously every Saturday with my family. Sure, this lot were probably better athletes, but did they possess the talent of Barnes, Rush, Grobbelaar and Beardsley. I wasn't sure. I guess it's one to be debated over the ages. All I knew is watching them there with my arl Fella and my brother beside me, meant they'd finally won a place in my heart beside that legendary title winning side who'd played under Dalglish. Like those legends, I knew I might not see them here again, but I knew I would be back. This was the only place to heal my wounds. The Kop, right here. This was my church. I'm not saying I'd found God. I probably couldn't even find Mo Salah with a five-yard pass if he was stood in front of an open goal. We all knew I couldn't catch a pig in a jigger. But even I had to admit somebody must've blessed that broken road which led me home.

They didn't present the trophy to the boys for another ten minutes. Certain things needed to be put in place. The lights

298

came up and with them a sobering feeling passed through my veins. I was definitely the only one standing in the Kop by then. But what a privilege it was to see Henderson lift the cup, surrounded by red streamers and ticker-tape. His teammates followed him up onto a makeshift stage, collecting their medals, one by one. They danced together, posing for photos and spraying each other with champagne. As the memory of standing beside my arl Fella faded into the night, that's when I realised, with ar T ozzle getting married in church, ar Wayne finding faith and my Ma agreeing to become an Elder, maybe, just maybe, that potty-mouthed, seed-sowing, Irishman, might just have achieved something with his final breath which he hadn't managed in his living years. He might just have saved us all. I was on my way home by the time I remembered about the match report. Truthfully, I'd only written four words. I was pretty sure I couldn't string them out into an article, but with a bit of work, I wondered if they could become a novel.

You'll Never Walk Alone.

Have you considered writing a review?

Tales From the Kop is an independent publisher competing in a world of multi-nationals. Whilst we have a small marketing budget, we find the best type of advertisement comes from our readers. So if you've enjoyed reading this book we'd really appreciate a review on Amazon.

Many thanks in advance from the whole team at,

Tales From The Kop

P.S. Tales From The Kop can be found on Facebook and Instagram with all the latest news and gossip regarding upcoming releases.

Acknowledgements

Tales from the Kop would like to extend a very warm and personal thanks to Ingrid Spiegl and the Scouse Press for granting permission to use Stan Kelly-Bootle's beautiful translation of Omar Khayyam's Rubaiyut. Not only is it a wonderful stand-alone piece, but it was amazing how sweetly it fitted with Wayne's story in You'll Never Walk Alone. For those interested in literature of a scouse persuasion please visit their website at www.scousepress.co.uk

Thanks to David Nicholls for helping with the cover design. For more information on his work please visit www.1079design.com

And finally…To everyone who has supported this project, you know who you are…YNWA!.

Printed in Great Britain
by Amazon